# *Broken Promises*

## A Past Imperfect Mystery

Between the Lines Publishing (USA)

410 Caribou Trail, Lutsen, Minnesota 55612, USA

www.btwnthelines.com

Cover Art: Artist Point, Grand Marais MN
by: Blaidd Photography

Broken Promises
A Past Imperfect Mystery

Paperback: 978-1-7321723-1-9
Also available in ebook format

Originally published as Broken Promises © 2017
ISBN: 978-0-9979395-4-5

To my amazing husband.
Thank you for listening to my crazy ideas and always
telling me to go for my dreams.

# ~ Chapter 1 ~

Julia tapped *Save*, closing her spreadsheet with a satisfied smile. Leaning back in the worn floral-patterned desk chair, her sapphire-blue eyes fell on the silver frame to her right. Collecting it, she sighed. "Well, we did it, Aunt Sadie. Two months along and the shop is still going strong." Her finger traced the older woman's face in the picture. Julia shared the same copper hair as her favorite aunt, though without the silvery gray streaks. Kissing the picture with a fingertip, Julia returned the frame to the desk. "I wouldn't be here if it wasn't for you. Though I'd much rather have you."

Beyond hair and eye color, Julia also shared her late aunt's love of the past. When Julia was just a young girl, she would venture off with her aunt to auctions and estate sales looking for bits of treasure. Sadie didn't have the antique shop then, but she enjoyed connecting with the past through the items they found. With each find,

Sadie made up a story, bringing the object's mysterious past to life. The rides home in her dark red 1932 Oldsmobile convertible, the rumble seat holding their treasures, were filled with romance, chivalry, and sometimes ghost stories. Sadie's laugh, like a soft spring rain, made Julia smile then, and the memory made her smile now. She sighed again, remembering how she'd lie on the dewy grass dreaming of one day living in an old Victorian house with a huge attic, leaded glass windows, and a grand staircase. Unfortunately, sometimes life doesn't turn out the way we dream.

The insistent jingle from the brass bell above the front door pulled Julia's attention. She brushed away an errant tear before heading to greet her customer. Her soft-soled suede boots scuffed along the pine floor, which was badly in need of refinishing. She thought the floor expressed the character of her antique shop, "Past Imperfect," well…perfectly. Her calf-length retro corded skirt brushed against a sideboard with a whitewash finish as she reached the front entrance. Her old-fashioned sense of style, while misplaced in the Cities, complimented the shop. Julia never felt comfortable in the latest looks, preferring flowy skirts, boots, and poet blouses. When her hair wasn't in a braid, she looked like a throwback to another time.

"Hello, welcome to Past Imperfect." Julia offered a warm smile to the older couple. Based on their clothing, she assumed they were tourists. Although Grand Marais was an artist-centered community, those who lived there year-round often opted for functionality over style. The tall, sun-kissed man gave a grin and a slightly accented *hello*, confirming her impression.

"The wife and I are headed home to Thunder Bay. We were passing through and decided to stop and explore."

The woman standing next to him curved her perfectly painted red lips into a smile. She reminded Julia of her mother. Olivia Branson never left the house without lipstick on. The woman before her was put together well, in a cream-colored linen pantsuit and soft pink blouse. Her posture and grace suggested she was a woman who knew what she wanted. "I don't know why we never stopped before. We've driven through so many times over the years." Her intense green eyes scanned the shop as she spoke, finding their intended target, she strolled away. "Mike, isn't this brilliant?" Her prey was a Victorian carved-oak cylinder secretary with a double-door bookcase hutch. Two etched-glass doors opened to expose a double-shelf interior. The top drawer curved elegantly with two flat drawers beneath and a single cupboard door above.

Mike followed, remarking on the desk. Julia learned early on not to oversell an item; customers generally knew what they liked and high pressures sales were not her style. A few moments into exploring the desk, the woman grinned with delight upon finding a small ink stain. Julia smiled, appreciating a fellow lover of the past. Mike glanced over at Julia and smiled. "We'll take it."

Mike followed Julia to her writer's desk, leaving his wife to discover any secret compartments often found in older furniture. Julia pulled the sales book from the desk drawer as Mike produced a checkbook. Julia smiled, asking quietly, "You don't want to know the price before you buy it?"

Mike's lips curled into a warm smile of understanding. "I only need to know that she's happy." Glancing at his checkbook, he added, "But I do need to know what to write the check out for." His eyes twinkled in a way that made Julia smile back. Internally, she hoped to one day find that kind of love.

Finishing up the sales receipt, Julia handed Mike his copy as the bell jingled again. She escorted him back to the front of the shop. Dan, the mail carrier, offered an easy smile, carried a small box tucked under his arm. "Just one package today."

Julia nodded. "I'll be right back. I just need to help load a desk."

Dropping the box and his electronic scanner on the sideboard, Dan shook his head. "I'll get it."

Julia watched the young man with thick biceps hoist the desk easily, carrying it out to the couple's sport utility vehicle.

Mike's wife flashed an appreciative smile at Julia, who felt the warmth of a blush color her cheeks. "He is handsome." Leaving the comment on the air, she stepped back into the afternoon sunshine with a soft chuckle.

Dan eased back into the shop, scanned the package, and collected Julia's signature. "See you tomorrow." He waved back over his shoulder.

Julia noticed the airmail stickers and customs documents on the front of the box. "Curious. I didn't order anything." The box was dented on one corner and smudged with dirt. Examining the customs documents didn't offer any further clues; the delicate paper was smeared from what looked like recent water damage. Julia could only make out that it came from somewhere in Paris. The date indicated it had left Paris six months earlier. Putting the paperwork aside, Julia looked at the address label. It was addressed to Sarah Walters. "Aunt Sadie." Julia touched the ink lightly as a sad smile teased her mouth.

Opening the package, Julia found a wooden box inside. Her heart tangoed; the mystery around an unexpected package always brought out childish curiosity. Sliding the small brass hook to one side, she opened it, relishing the singular moment of discovery.

Inside the decorative box, nestled on crushed crimson velvet, was an object hidden in a matching velvet sleeve. She slipped on a pair of white curator gloves and lifted the treasure from its nest, carefully sliding the sleeve off to reveal a silver letter opener. The blade was embellished with a plethora of repoussé scrollwork and a pierced lattice end surrounded by floral motifs. Turning the blade over, Julia discovered the initials E.C. etched at the base near the edge of the handle. She smiled. "If I'm not mistaken, eighteenth century and very English." Her gloved finger traced over the initials. Julia's aunt's voice sang out softly, and a grand story of the owner started to play in her mind.

"That's beautiful."

Julia jumped at the unexpected voice behind her. Turning, she let out a breath of relief. "Lucy, you startled me. I didn't hear you come in."

Lucy's normal large brown eyes widened. "I can see that."

Julia looked down and realized she was holding the letter opener like a weapon. She set it back inside the box and stripped off her white cotton gloves. Turning back to Lucy, she said, "Sorry, I'm just a bit jumpy today."

Lucy's demeanor relaxed and bright smile returned, accepting the answer without question. Nothing ever seemed to bother her. Her upbeat nature was nice to have around, especially when Julia first arrived in Grand Marais. She hired Lucy from the community college to help part-time in the shop. The few hours Lucy worked each week gave Julia a chance to get out and enjoy the afternoon sun during the less crowded weekdays. Lucy Wells dropped her pink backpack beside the desk. "Why don't you take a break? I'll look after things."

"That'd be great." Julia's skirt brushed the edge of the box, sending it and its contents crashing to the floor. "Damn it." Julia stooped down to clean up the mess, grasping the letter opener bare-handed while she searched for its protective sleeve. While she was leaned over, a touch of vertigo struck her, and a fragment of memory came to mind like something out a dream. She could see a room decorated in pristine eighteenth-century furniture and then a woman's hands caressing the roundness of her belly. And then blood...so much *blood.*

"*Julia...*"

Julia nearly smacked her head on the desk as she broke from her reverie. She knew that dreams from the previous night could surface in her mind throughout the day, triggered by some reminder, but she had never experienced a dream like this, so real and palpable. It was so believable she'd almost thought she could smell the blood—like a handful of old pennies—as it dripped from her hands.

"Hang on," Julia called from under the desk, where she spotted the sleeve and carefully fitted it back over the ornate handle. She placed it back in its box, noticing a bit of folded paper concealed beneath. Julia removed the paper before returning the letter opener and closing the wooden box. Straightening up, she slipped the note into the pocket of her skirt and asked, "What did you say?"

Lucy was several feet away, rummaging around in the broom closet. "Hmm?" She looked over her shoulder, confused. "I didn't say anything."

"I thought you called my name," Julia said, furrowing her brow while touching her temples. The vertigo had passed, replaced now with an eerie sense of dread. *You're hearing things.* Brushing it off, she agreed with Lucy's suggestion. "I think a break is just the thing I need right now." She opened the desk drawer. "I'll check this in when I get back." Julia grabbed her purse and Aunt Sadie's favorite fedora from the desk drawer, replacing them with the box. "Can I bring anything back for you?"

"No thanks, I'm good," Lucy sang out, her blond ponytail swinging as she grabbed a dusting rag and moved deeper into the shop. Julia liked Lucy, hoping one day she might be able to afford her on a full-time basis.

Julia slung her bag onto her shoulder, sniffing a gentle floral scent in the air. "Is that a new perfume?"

"Do you like it?" Lucy's voice carried over the various displays. "My mom gave it to me for my birthday. I think she's finally seeing that I'm not a kid anymore."

Julia chuckled. "I understand completely. It's always hard for parents, especially mothers with their daughters. It's lovely – very mature." She had one hand on the door. "Well, I shouldn't be gone long; I have a couple of errands to run after lunch."

"Don't worry about anything. It's a beautiful day, so enjoy the sun."

Julia headed out. Past Imperfect, located in an older brick building across the street from the Shoreline Motel and next door to Beth's Fudge and Gifts, was just a short walk from Wisconsin Street. She waved to Brian as he opened Sydney's Custard for the afternoon. The side street was quiet now, but by Thursday it would be bustling with tourists arriving to enjoy the annual late summer music festival. Continuing along Broadway, Julia cut through the bank parking lot on the corner; she paused, enjoying the new window display at the Siverston Gallery. She took delight in dealing with antiquities, but she favored the local artists for the walls of her one-bedroom flat above the shop.

Adam came out of the gallery, bucket and squeegee in hand. Besides managing the gallery, Adam headed up the arts council. "Afternoon, Julia. How's things at the shop?"

Julia smiled. "Great. Quiet today, but that only makes it easier to enjoy a gorgeous day like this." Her eyes fell on a piece of carved copper hanging in the window. "That's lovely. Is it new?"

"As a matter of fact, I just finished putting up the display. The artist uses copper to create the carvings. The one with the tree along the shore is my favorite."

"It's amazing. I know the perfect spot for it."

Adam dropped his window cleaning supplies and held the door open. "Step into my parlor and see what treasures we have." He offered his trademark laid-back smile as the afternoon breeze teased his brown hair. Although Adam had come to Grand Marais two years earlier, he still looked like a surfer who just stepped off some beach in southern California.

Inside the gallery, Julia admired the various pieces on display, all created by local artists. Along the back wall, Adam had the rest of the copper pieces hanging. All of them were intricately carved, but the tree seemed to call to Julia. "I'll take it. Would you mind delivering it to the shop when you get a chance?"

"Not at all. I'll drop it by when Connor gets back from Lutsen later today."

"A little early for skiing, isn't it?" Julia teased. Connor was Adam's partner in the gallery and in life. Adam had the talent for art and Connor handled the business side. Together they created a successful artists' co-op of a sort.

Adam's green eyes twinkled. "This is for the new resort. He's hoping to get the contract to supply the artwork for the guest suites."

"Wonderful. I hope it works out. I wonder if they could use a few antiques in the lobby?" Julia mused as she tucked the receipt into her bag. "Say 'hi' to Connor for me." Julia headed out of the gallery towards the next shop.

Pushing the glass door open, Julia entered the Blue Water Café and smiled when she saw the ever-present coffee klatch gathered at their usual center table. They were a close-knit group of people who seemed to know everything that went on in town. They were just one of the many things she loved about Grand Marais. Julia had been in town for almost a month before she was invited to join them. That morning, she found herself accepted by the community of artisans. Julia waved at Jacob, who motioned her over.

"Good afternoon, lovely lady. How's it going at the shop?" He offered a wide, infectious grin.

Julia returned it. "Great. I just popped in for a bit of lunch."

"Then I'll save a seat for you for next time."

"I promise to take you up on it." Seeing her favorite booth was empty, Julia squeezed Jacob's shoulder before heading back. Jacob Prescott was one of the sweetest people Julia knew. He was one of the first artists to settle in the small town on the shores of Lake Superior. Forty years later, the town was a well-known artist community that tourists flocked to each summer for the many festivals, fall for the spectacular colors, winter for the skiing, and spring when life sprouted forth, showing that the world would once again be warm. It made perfect sense; Lake Superior had been a year-round draw for the area for almost a century.

Settling down on the dark blue vinyl seat, Julia passed on looking at the menu. The café was one of her favorite places to enjoy lunch, and they made a mean BLT club she'd been thinking about all morning. The décor's theme was shipping. On the far wall was a mural of Lake Superior with markers indicating shipwrecks. The lake was famous for ships both on the water and beneath the surface. On the wall where Julia sat were photographs of famous ships, including the Edmund Fitzgerald, the large ore ship that had sunk during a November gale storm. Although the décor focused on the tragedies on the lake, it also showed the town's proud past and how important commercial shipping was in its creation.

Several minutes passed without anyone stopping by the table. That was unusual. Emily and Sandy never let a customer wait more than a minute before greeting them and offering coffee, no matter how busy the café was. Other than the coffee klatch, Julia was the only customer.

Julia spied Emily Peterson exiting the kitchen, a frown tugged at the corners of her mouth. Her chestnut-brown hair was pulled back in a hasty ponytail. Emily grabbed the kettle of hot water and filled a small ceramic teapot before heading over to Julia.

"Sorry for the delay. Tea, right?" Emily placed the antique porcelain pot, decorated with tiny pink roses, on the table. Julia's tea was always served in it.

"Perfect." Julia liked the idea of having a teapot of her own at the café. It made her feel like a true part of the community. Glancing up, she asked, "How are things?" Julia noticed Emily staring at the large front window, though she couldn't see what had her attention. "Emily?"

Emily jerked her head back to Julia as if she'd been slapped. "I'm sorry. I didn't catch that." She pulled out her order pad.

"Are you all right? You seem distracted."

"I'm fine. What can I get for you?" Emily offered curtly.

Unfamiliar dark circles and puffy eyes suggested otherwise. "Just the BLT Club."

"Okay, and what kind of cheese?" Emily asked, glancing at the window again.

"On a BLT?" Now Julia knew something was wrong.

"BLT? I thought you wanted a cheeseburger." She scratched out the order, rewriting it. "I'm so sorry. My mind just isn't here today."

Julia smiled sympathetically. "It's okay. You look exhausted. Is there anything I can do?"

Emily's dark brown eyes glistened. "Thanks, but I don't want to bother you."

Reaching up, Julia touched Emily's bare forearm gently. "It isn't a bother. That's what friends are for."

Sighing, she replied, "I'll put your order in and be right back." She turned, her sneakers squeaking as she took the few steps to the counter and stretched up, clipping the order sheet to the metal wheel.

Over the past month, Julia had grown to consider Emily Peterson a friend. They met the first time Julia stopped by the café. She'd arrived two weeks before but had found herself deep in grief and working through Sadie's things that she'd never taken a stroll through town. Later that same afternoon, Emily had come by the shop and looked around. She finally settled on a small porcelain teapot, the one that Julia now used every time she ate at the café. It was the sweetest gesture of welcome anyone had ever given her. It was after that day the coffee klatch offered her a seat. Julia was appreciative of the kindness she'd been shown and wanted to help Emily any way she could.

She watched as Emily grabbed a cup of coffee before heading back towards the table. She paused when the glass café door swung open and a man stepped in. Emily put the cup down. "Here's your coffee. The rest of your order will be right up." She offered a small smile, then stepped over to the man.

He looked to be in his mid- to late thirties, tall and lean with wavy black hair and a cultivated beard. He was handsome, in a mountain man sort of way. Julia's brow furrowed as the man escorted Emily outside, his hand gripping her elbow. She couldn't hear them, but it was obvious their conversation wasn't a pleasant one. Emily's arms flailed with anger, and the man's lip curled indignantly. The couple pulled at memories of Julia's own relationship experience, still too painfully fresh for her liking.

A plate appeared on the table in front of Julia, as Sandy shot her a smile. She was far more attentive than

Emily had been, but even so, Julia could see she was distracted by the same argument going on outdoors as well. "Who is that with Emily?" Julia asked out of impolite curiosity.

Sandy snorted. "That's her husband, Tom."

"Doesn't sound like you like him much."

Another snort as Sandy shook her head. "Not much to like."

Julia wanted to ask why, but Emily came back in, wiping her eyes as she hurried past and disappeared into the kitchen.

Sandy bolted from Julia's table, trailing off after Emily with a troubled look on her face.

Left alone, Julia glanced back out the window just in time to see Emily's husband forcefully kicking the tire of his truck with one heavy-duty work boot. He then flopped into the driver's seat of the GMC with wild, exaggerated anger before slamming the door and squealing away.

# Broken Promises

# ~ Chapter 2 ~

Lucy slid open the large desk drawer, wanting to steal a peek at the letter opener again. She knew she should wait for Julia, but she couldn't help herself. It was almost as if it were drawing her to it like a magnetic piece of art. It was beautiful, and she couldn't help herself. She thought Julia had amazing taste in everything she did and wanted to learn all she could from her. So much so that Lucy added Art History to her next term of classes. Holding the letter opener by the velvet-covered handle, Lucy carefully turned it from one side to the other. Julia must have been flustered when she put the opener away—she'd left the blade exposed. "E.C., I wonder who you were." Placing a finger at the tip, Lucy turned it so she could see the etching more clearly.

"What'cha looking at, honey?"

Startled, Lucy dropped the opener onto the desk and turned to the familiar voice. "Nothing. Why did you sneak up on me?" Lucy snapped.

"Honey, why are you so jumpy?"

Taken aback by her own curt response, she replied, "I'm sorry. I just didn't hear you come in." Guilt laced her tone.

The woman shook her teased blond head. "Lucille Marie Wells, I'm your mother; I think I know when you're jumpy." Heavy high heels echoed along the wooden floor as Lucy's mother closed the short distance, pulling her into a hug. "Tell me what's going on. You never snap at anyone."

Lucy returned the hug, brushing off her out-of-character response as being startled. "Why so dressed up in the middle of the day?" Lucy shifted the subject, though she didn't have to ask; she knew the answer all too well.

Dottie Cooper smoothed down her curve-hugging leather miniskirt and smiled. "I'm meeting Pete."

Lucy's nose wrinkled. Her mother had been dating Pete for about a month, and Lucy still hadn't met him. She looked at the revealing blouse and ceiling-high heels. Lucy shook internally; she didn't understand what was going on with her mother. Before she and her father had divorced two years prior, Dottie was a typical soccer mom. One day, Lucy came home from high school to find her father putting suitcases in the cab of his truck. Lucy never knew what really happened, only that her mother said he didn't want them anymore, took back her maiden name, and now, the ponytails and jeans were replaced with tight, cleavage-revealing clothes. "Mom, will I ever meet this Pete?"

Checking her look in a nearby Hallandale oval wall mirror, Dottie touched up her Ruby Woo by MAC lipstick. "Don't worry, sweetie. I want to make sure he's the *one* before getting you involved." Stepping back over to Lucy, she said, "Now, don't pout. You know it's been hard since your father left. Now, come on, let me see that beautiful smile."

Lucy couldn't help but feel wary over this mysterious *Pete*, especially since her mother was behaving in such a secretive manner. *What is it about this man that she's so afraid of me discovering?* she wondered, conjuring up images of tattoos and arrest records. Lucy sighed into her toes and acquiesced. She wouldn't get the answers she wanted until her mother was ready.

Dottie's ruby lips curled up. "That's my girl." She tapped a red-polished nail on Lucy's cheek. "Don't worry so much. Pete is a wonderful guy, and when the time is right, I promise you'll meet him. There are a couple of things he needs to deal with before that can happen, but I promise it will. Okay?"

The comment only made Lucy more suspicious, but she knew there was really no arguing with her mother, especially lately, so she just nodded and held the expected smile.

"So, what is that?" Dottie motioned to the letter opener on the desk.

"Oh, it's nothing. Julia just got this in the mail, and I was looking at it." The front door opened, and a young couple walked in. "I'll be right back." Lucy left her mother at the desk to tend to the customers.

The couple headed to the corner where the smaller antiques were kept. Lucy remembered Julia saying that it was always good to have little treasures for customers to discover. Not all sales could be large, and it was often the hunt for tiny treasures that brought newcomers in the door.

"Hi, welcome to Past Imperfect. Is there anything special you're looking for today?" Lucy had to admit that she was happy to have a break from her mother and interacting with the customers was one of her favorite parts of the job.

"It'll sound silly, but I collect salt and pepper shakers. Nothing normal—the kitschy kind. Do you have anything like that?"

"Well, we have a few sets, found at various estate sales. They're right over here, in the corner." Lucy walked the couple over to the cabinet stocked with shakers—incongruous pairs of owls, matte-finished mice, and even a little elderly ceramic couple.

Lucy looked on with satisfaction when the young woman squealed in delight as she examined a brightly painted set in the shape of a rooster and hen.

As the couple chatted, Lucy thought she heard something fall in the back of the shop. "If there's anything I can help you with, just yell." She excused herself and made her way back to the desk. "Mom?"

"Sugar, I need to go." Dottie's manicured hand rested impatiently on her hip.

"Everything okay? I thought I heard something fall."

Dottie shrugged. "Just knocked a book off the desk. Now, I really need to get going."

"Okay, I'll see you at home later?" Lucy knew the answer but couldn't help asking.

Dottie didn't respond; she only hugged her daughter again, being careful not to smudge her makeup or crush her perfectly teased curls. Turning, Dottie strutted out of the shop, her stiletto heels echoing along the wooden floor.

Once she was gone, Lucy scanned the desk. She found the letter opener still out on the surface, but the velvet sheath wasn't there. "No...no..." Lucy looked all over the desk in a fluster of nerves. "Come on; you have to be here." In her agitated state, she knocked a pen off the side and stooped down to collect it, irritation at her mother growing. Just under the desk, she found the missing piece of velvet, relief flooded her senses. Lucy snatched the polishing cloth Julia kept in the top drawer and carefully wiped the fine silver blade clean.

"I'd like to buy this set," the customer said, placing the rooster and the hen gingerly on the desk.

Lucy slipped the cover over the ornate handle, stashed it back in its box, and returned it to the desk drawer before ringing up the purchase.


Julia stepped out of the Gunflint Mercantile carrying her bag of soup mixes and half-pound of peanut butter chocolate fudge. The Mercantile sold everything from packaged dry soup mixes and homemade fudge to hard candy and tourist trinkets. Julia's favorite was the Cream of Chicken and Wild Rice soup. Minnesota was famous for wild rice, and this soup came closest to her own homemade. Strolling through town after finishing her lunch, Julia wasn't ready to go back to Past Imperfect. She was sure she was taking advantage of Lucy's generous nature, but seeing Emily upset and arguing with her husband had reminded Julia of her own relationship failures. Crossing the street to Birchbark Books & Gifts, Julia peeked in the large front window. Spying a lavender sweater on display just inside, she reached for the door, deciding a little shopping therapy wasn't a bad thing.

An hour later, she was back at her desk, opening the inventory log to enter the letter opener. Pulling up several antiques databases, Julia searched the images for the ornate filigree handle without any luck. Frustration pricked at her. She knew it couldn't be sold for its proper value without provenance, and so far, the mystery of where the letter opener originated refused to be solved.

Julia glanced up at the sound of the front bell ringing. She started to rise, but hearing Lucy greet the customer sent her back to the search. She picked up the opener to study the handle. "What little secrets are you hiding?"

"Julia?"

Startled, she turned, surprised to find Emily standing next to the bookcase Julia used as a wall to create the small office space. "Emily. Hi. I thought you were a customer. What can I do for you?"

"I'm sorry; I didn't mean sneak up on you. I was hoping we could talk, but..." Emily hesitated, biting her lip to hold back tears. "Never mind. You're obviously busy and I shouldn't bother you."

"No...no. Wait. It's not a bother. Um...why don't we go upstairs and chat?"

Emily looked relieved. "I'd like that."

Julia offered a reassuring smile and led Emily to the staircase leading to the upstairs flat. "Lucy, would you mind watching the shop? We'll just be upstairs."

"Sure, no problem," Lucy called back from the front of the shop.

Julia led the way up the bare first few steps before turning on the small landing to head up the remaining flight. The bottom three steps were replaced after Julia took over the shop and hadn't been finished yet. The rest still bore the dark natural finish from the original build. When Julia opened the door to her home, there was a streak of orange as her cat, King Henry, ran for cover at the sight of a newcomer. "How about a cup of tea—or would you prefer something stronger? I have some wine in the fridge."

"As much as I'd like the wine, I need to get home in a bit to have dinner ready when Tom gets home."

Julia nodded. "Tea it is." Heading into the kitchen area, Julia set the kettle to boil, then joined Emily in the living room.

"I never knew there was an apartment above your shop. I just assumed it was storage."

"It's not much, but I love it. I can sit on the roof and watch the lake and the tourists searching for agates." Julia headed to the kitchen when the kettle whistled. "It's also nice not to have far to go to work." The boiling water cascaded gently over the tea balls. Taking her seat again, Julia offered a cup to Emily, who seemed grateful to have something to do with her hands.

"Thank you." Emily cradled the cup in her lap, staring at the steam wafting up.

Julia didn't want to push her into conversation before she was ready, so she sipped on her tea, trying not to stare.

"I think Tom is having an affair," Emily burst out, cutting the thick silence. She wouldn't look up; instead, her fingers played nervously over the edge of the cup.

Julia let out a quiet breath. She didn't know what to say, only slightly relieved it wasn't something like abuse. Earlier, she'd noticed what looked like a bruise on Emily's forearm, and in the pit of her stomach, she had feared the worst. "Are you certain?"

Emily's head bobbed up and down, something about her sadness made her seem young and vulnerable. "He gets phone calls at odd hours, then leaves the room to have the conversation. When I ask who it was, he tells me it's just work, no big deal. If it was no big deal, why leave the room? Tom works in sales, so I don't know why he'd get business calls at night. After that, he started keeping his phone on him, even when he gets home. Last week he was late getting home from work. His shirt smelled of flowery perfume. I've never worn flower-scented perfume in my life." The words tumbled from her mouth all at once.

Reaching over, Julia captured Emily's hand gently. "Could there be another explanation? Maybe he was shopping for you. You know how the perfume counter is." Julia didn't believe her own suggestion but wanted desperately to help.

Emily squeezed Julia's fingers before pulling back. Quickly wiping an errant tear, she continued, "That's not all."

Julia braced herself, thinking again of the bruise on Emily's forearm coupled with the anger Tom had shown outside the restaurant. She wondered if her relief might have come a little too soon.

Emily leaned in closer. "I did the laundry this morning and found lipstick on his collar—and to top it off, we received a credit card statement for a card I didn't know he had." Tears glistened again, her voice catching. "There were charges to restaurants in Thunder Bay and Victoria's Secret. Tom has never bought me anything from Victoria's Secret. I didn't even know he knew how to buy lingerie."

Julia's stomach tightened. Everything Emily said reminded her of her husband, Graham. He had always said he loved her, but Julia knew he enjoyed the attention he got from younger women in great excess. Of course, he'd promised her it was just harmless flirtations. Even if that were true, the hurt it caused was destructive, especially when the interns Graham worked with were all college students, younger and prettier—at least in Julia's eyes. Hearing Emily's voice break again wrenched Julia back to the present.

"We ended up getting into a huge fight over it. I started to walk out to go to work, and he grabbed at me to stop me from leaving." Emily vaguely touched her arm at the spot where the bluish-purple mark had formed.

"You can't stay with him," Julia blurted out, for a moment unconcerned how overbearing it might come across.

Emily's eyes widened as a frown pulled the corners of her mouth down. She looked at her cup in silence, her fingers still fidgeting with the handle.

Julia felt the heat of a blush. "I'm sorry. I shouldn't have said that." Taking a sip of her tea, she collected herself. "What do *you* want to do? If you need a place to stay, you are more than welcome to stay with me." She offered a reassuring smile. "It's not much, but I'd be happy to have you."

Emily looked up with open surprise. "Thank you for that. You're sweet." She took a breath. "I plan on talking to him about it tonight. One way or the other, it's going to be dealt with."

"Promise me two things, will you?" Julia handed Emily the embroidered linen handkerchief she always kept in her pocket.

"What?" Emily sniffed and dried the tears that threatened to fall.

"First, that you'll be careful. Things could blow up easily over infidelity."

Emily narrowed her eyes. "Tom would never hurt me," she protested. "Not like that. But I'll be careful. So, what's the second thing?"

"Promise to stop by the store in the morning to let me know you're okay."

Emily offered a surprised but warm smile. "I promise to stop by on my way to work."

"Great." Julia smiled, relieved. She pulled Emily into a hug and beamed when she returned it.

# Broken Promises

# ~ Chapter 3 ~

Julia spent the rest of the afternoon trying not to think of how much Emily's husband reminded her of her own ex—well, future ex-husband. She hadn't heard anything since filing the divorce papers. *Maybe he hasn't been served yet.* Julia decided to sit on the deck just off her kitchen, enjoying the cool evening air. It wasn't so much a balcony as it was the rooftop of the storage building on the back of the shop. Julia had lined the edges with fragrant plants and flowers, an outdoor area rug, and two chairs with a small table, all of which gave it a homey feeling. Easing back against the wooden Adirondack chair, she tried to let go of the day. It didn't take long for the sound of the breaking waves from the lake to start easing the tension.

The sound of Kelly Clarkson singing about an ex-boyfriend called from the kitchen; the tension roared back. Climbing out of the chair, Julia headed inside. Her fingers played nervously over her lips as she stared at the incoming call screen. *Graham*. He was the last person she wanted to speak to. She knew he wouldn't be happy getting served with divorce papers and would make certain she knew it. Biting on her thumbnail, a habit she picked up during her marriage, Julia reached for the phone. "I can't put this off," she said aloud to steel her nerves, but the ringing stopped just as she slid the arrow to accept. She blew out a long breath she didn't know she was holding.

King Henry jumped onto the counter, brushing against her and demanding attention. She scratched him behind his misshapen ear, a war wound from his days as a homeless wanderer on the streets. He reminded Julia of Henry VIII, with his burnt-orange fur, stout body, and kingly manner. "Maybe he gave up." Julia kissed the top of his head as the familiar sound of a new voicemail message rang out. She sighed. "I can't get that lucky." Grabbing the phone, she tapped the voicemail icon. Listening on speakerphone, feeling like it would somehow keep him at a greater distance, she heard Graham's voice come on the line.

*"Juls...Look, I know you were upset with me. You had every right to be, but all that's over with. I made a mistake. Baby, I don't want to lose you. We were...are good together.*

*You've taken time for yourself, but I think it's time you came back home. We can talk everything over. I'm not going to give up on us...ever. I love you."*

Hearing the pain in his voice brought pangs of guilt for filing the papers without talking to him first. "He didn't deserve that." King Henry meowed in response. Julia looked at his round face. "What, you think he deserved it? I know, I'm being soft, aren't I? He didn't talk to me before having an affair with that intern." Scooping Henry up, she headed to the oversized chair in the living room. She sank back against the embroidered pillows, snuggling Henry onto her lap. Graham's message repeated in her mind.

He was never openly mean or cruel in any way, but those offenses would have been too obvious. Their friends all thought he was the perfect husband. He was handsome, meticulous with his clothes, well-educated — they met in college. Their friends, more like his friends, didn't know the same man she did. Her best friend, Tina, was the only one who ever said a word against him. From that first meeting in the student union, Tina tried to warn Julia off him, but she wouldn't listen. Julia was in love and at first, their relationship was wonderful. She smiled anytime she saw him, and butterflies filled her when his name came on her caller ID. If she were honest about it, things weren't as wonderful as she made herself believe. Even in college Graham had a way of making Julia question everything. After being accepted as a graduate student by the art history department of Columbia, Graham helped her celebrate with a party, but within a few days he started dropping little comments against her going to New York. He would wait until they were cuddled together, then whisper about being worried for her in a dangerous city like New York. Those comments shifted to ones about being apart and being lonely. By the end of the same month, she'd reversed her acceptance and accepted a place with him at Cal State. At the time, she had even forced herself to believe it was her own decision—but, Graham was the one who loved the beach and wanted to spend as much time there as possible. And once they were there, he did.

Julia snorted a soft chuckle. The irony was not lost on her that she lived just yards from the largest freshwater lake and Graham lived inland. His voicemail tugged at familiar cords. During their fifteen-year marriage, Graham whittled away at Julia, carving and smoothing her into something resembling the wife that he wanted. As time went on, she felt she had little in common with her true self; the disagreements from the early years of their marriage, when she had still tried standing up for what she wanted, became distant memories. If she were completely honest, she grew tired of fighting. Calls made in search of support to her mother or sister never ended well. They only saw him as witty or charming.

Once they relocated to the Twin Cities, Julia found ways to have time for herself. Graham never liked working in the yard, so she found a gardening center along with a large farmer's market. They gave Julia a lifeline to herself and her marriage. Her degree sat in a moving box collecting dust while Graham worked. His job had allowed for her to stay at home, which was exactly how he liked it. He didn't care how she spent her day, never bothering to ask, as long as she had dinner ready when he got home.

Henry gave her an irritated purr when she stopped petting him. Shaking away the past, she said tartly, "I'm sorry. I shouldn't ignore you." With another snort, Julia realized she'd traded one dominating male for another. "At least you're loyal." The large cat climbed up on her chest with his front paws, bumping his forehead against her jaw. Julia hugged him before kissing him on the head. "My sweet boy." He snuggled back onto her lap, purring contentedly as she stroked his back. She shifted a bit to get comfortable, grabbing the book from the table to her right, as she and Henry enjoyed the quiet.

A loud crash sent Julia bolting upright. She looked around, disoriented, but her apartment seemed all right. Through sleep-filled eyes, she glanced at the clock on the kitchen wall. Two a.m. Rubbing the heel of her hand over her eyes, she looked again. "Must have fallen asleep." A second crash from downstairs shook her. Julia's already pounding heart leapt into her throat. *Someone is in the shop.* Moving as quietly as possible, she made her way to the kitchen. Taking her phone, she dialed 9-1-1. When the operator came on, she whispered, "Yes, this is Julia Crawford at Past Imperfect." Her eyes darted towards the open door leading down to the shop.

"Ma'am?"

The concerned voice on the other end of the phone pulled Julia back. "I'm sorry. Yes, I live in the apartment above the antique shop. I think someone has broken in." Her voice betrayed the fear she felt in her heart.

"Mrs. Crawford, this is Michelle. We met at the book festival last month."

"Y…yes, I remember."

"I've dispatched a deputy to your location. He's five minutes from you. Is it safe for you to stay where you are?"

Remembering the open entry door to her flat, Julia moved over to it, trying not to step on one of the loose boards. Peering through the door, she didn't see anything; the shop below was dark. Stepping back, she replied, "I think so."

"All right," Michelle's voice soothed. "I'm going to stay on the line until Sam gets there."

Julia let out a shaky breath. "Th—thank you." Falling against the wall, she held the phone close, listening to Michelle talk to her. A red strobe light lit up the street below. Julia moved quickly to the window and let out a breath. "He's here."

"Good. I'll hang up now. Have a good night."

"Thank you, Michelle; you too." Relieved, Julia headed down the stairs into the shop.

"Mrs. Crawford?" A bright flashlight shone in Julia's face.

"Yes. Sam?" Julia shielded her eyes from the intense beam.

The light dropped. "Yep, it's Deputy Reynolds." He was standing in the entryway of the shop.

Julia released her white-knuckle grip on the phone. "Am I glad to see you." She flipped the light switch up, flooding the shop with artificial light.

Deputy Reynolds looked no older than 25, with sandy blond hair and green eyes. His upper body filled his uniform shirt with little room to spare. Julia was happy to have the linebacker in her shop. He gave her an easy smile. "Let's take a look around." The hint of a southern heritage wove through his words, and the effect was calming.

"A crashing sound woke me from a dead sleep," Julia recounted as she followed Sam around the shop. He motioned for her to wait while he peered under furniture and inside closets, one hand making a fist around the tail of the flashlight and the other resting on his gun holster.

From behind the divider bookcase, the deputy called out to her, "I think I found your intruder. What about this fella?"

Julia stepped around the deputy, eager to see who had invaded her shop. "Henry?" Julia's cat was lying regally in his favorite spot on the desk, and the lamp was on the floor below.

"He must have knocked it off." Deputy Reynolds replaced the lamp, kindly straightening out the shade.

"Doesn't seem to be broken." Looking around, he asked, "Notice anything else missing or out of place?"

Julia examined the area, and everything looked just as she'd left it. A warm flush of embarrassment colored her cheeks as the fear wore off and reality set in. "I feel like such an idiot. I'm sorry to have dragged you out here."

"Don't worry about that, ma'am," the deputy assured her in his soothing tone. "Do you remember locking your door?"

"Of course. Actually..." Julia hesitated, trying hard to remember. The day before was fuzzy in her mind and falling asleep on in the oversized chair in her living room had thrown off her schedule. "No, I don't *specifically* remember locking it. It's such a habit, though, I can't imagine I would leave it open."

"Well, it was unlocked when I arrived," the deputy pointed out in a flat voice that wasn't accusing or excusing. "I'll take a report for the call. If you do have any trouble in the future, at least we'll have something on file."

Julia nodded, unable to shake the foolish-little-girl feeling. "Thank you for coming. I feel like I've wasted your time." She walked to the door with Sam.

"Don't worry about it. I'll drive past the shop a few more times tonight so you can get some sleep." Before leaving, Sam reminded her, "Just make sure to lock the door after me."

Julia nodded, closing and locking the door behind him. "You're in big trouble, mister," she said, scooping Henry into her arms. She switched off the lights and carried the furry bundle upstairs. "I should have had Sam arrest you," Julia teased as she closed and locked her apartment door as well, taking Henry to bed.

# Broken Promises

# ~ Chapter 4 ~

Julia woke from a restless night's sleep. She'd tossed and turned so much that Henry had given up on sleeping beside her and stalked out of the room, as if he were the one who should be mad at her after that lamp fiasco. It had been too hard to settle down after the break-in scare and Graham's voicemail, and what little sleep she did get had been consumed by nightmares. Now she was faced with the blinking amber light on her phone that indicated a text message waited. Sliding the phone on, she dared to hope it was Emily making good on her promise, saying everything was all right and that she would be over soon, but the text message wasn't from her; it was from Graham.

*"We need to talk. Call me."*

The curt message seemed less desperate than his voicemail. This one could be read as irritated or angry—

not surprising, knowing him. Julia rubbed her temples. "I can't deal with you now," she told her phone with a groan as she climbed out of bed and padded to the kitchen. Henry mewed, appealing for his breakfast. "Don't worry, your majesty, your repast is coming." Julia shook her head as she filled his bowl. "Too many demanding men in my life." She plunked the bowl on his mat.

Julia filled the kettle before placing it on the burner, then headed back to the bedroom to get ready for the day. Glancing at the clock, she saw she had time to shower and dress before Emily was due to stop by.

Less than an hour later, she sat on the deck, watching the water, enjoying her tea. As much as she loved working in her antique shop, she treasured Sunday mornings on the roof watching the water. It was the one day of the week Past Imperfect was closed, and it offered its own unique gifts. The slow ease of the day, the quiet whispers of the tide playing over the rocks near Artists' Point, and the squeals of children finding bits of agate scattered along the shore.

Julia watched a young couple walking along the beach holding hands, and it brought back memories of Graham. Not the later years, but the early days when they first started dating. During that time, he had swept her off her feet and placed her on a cloud. Unfortunately, so high a pedestal blinded her to reality. She watched until they were out of sight, refusing to give in to the threatening sadness. Henry came out, rubbed against her leg, and jumped from the deck to the roof below. He was off to explore until his stomach brought him home again.

Hearing the wall clock chime nine, Julia headed to the kitchen. She checked her phone, then put her teacup in the sink. Her stomach twisted into a knot when she didn't see a message from Emily. *Could she have forgotten about her promise?* Julia's fingers played over her lips apprehensively. She couldn't get rid of the nagging feeling that something was wrong. She sent Emily a text—*Are we still on for this morning?* —and then tried to busy herself around the apartment.

Julia managed to putter around for thirty whole minutes before her nerves couldn't take it anymore. She looked up Emily's address, pulled her sweater on, and locked the door behind her. She walked along Broadway through the business area of town. The streets were turning quiet with the end of the summer tourist season approaching. The change of temperature would bring another type of tourist altogether, one searching for amazing autumn colors. Julia looked forward to seeing the Gunflint Trail splashed in all the hues nature had on her palette. As she walked the few blocks along Wisconsin Street, the beauty of autumn seemed far in the future. The nagging concern with Emily kept Julia's thoughts rooted in the past, her mind replaying scenes of marital failures.

It wasn't until she bumped into a stranger that her mind focused on the present. "I'm so sorry."

The woman waved it off forgivingly, giving a friendly nod before heading on her way.

*Get it together, Juls.* She took a deep, centering breath as she trekked onward. It was just as she was turning the corner to walk up 3rd Avenue that she spotted Lucy and her bright pink backpack. "Lucy!" Julia called out, waving to her, but Lucy didn't seem to notice. Instead, her pace appeared to increase as she disappeared along 1st Street.

Julia brushed it off as she turned up 3rd Avenue West, figuring the girl must have been lost in her thoughts or wearing headphones that Julia simply hadn't noticed. Two blocks later, she turned left onto West 2nd Street, checking the addresses on the houses as she made her way. Spying the number on the mailbox for the house with blue siding on the cross-corner, she walked towards it where it stood nestled behind a tall row of pine bushes. Stopping in the intersection, her breath caught seeing the lights from the sheriff's car and an ambulance. *"Emily."* Fear crashed over her like a rocky avalanche. She bolted through the intersection, running towards Emily's house.

Movement from the house halted her steps. Julia watched as two men dressed in EMT uniforms wheeled a gurney outside, the body atop covered completely by a blood-stained sheet. Julia's hand flew up to her mouth, bile burning the back of her throat. She watched as they continued along the driveway to the waiting ambulance.

It took several beats, but finding her courage, Julia willed her feet to move. "Emily?" She ran the short distance. "No." Her progress was frozen by strong male arms clad in dark brown with gold-rimmed patches on the shoulder sleeves.

"You can't go any closer," his firm voice cautioned her while his large hands clamped firmly onto her biceps.

Julia tried to snatch her arms back reflexively. "Let me go! I just want to see to my friend."

"You knew the victim?" the sheriff asked, his grip unwavering.

Julia's shoulders dropped, her eyes refusing to leave the sight of the EMTs closing the ambulance doors. "It's my fault," she moaned as tears stung at the back of her eyes.

"How is it your fault, Julia?"

Hearing her addressed in the familiar, Julia looked up and into the deep brown eyes of Sheriff Jack Barrett. She was so distraught she hadn't even registered it was him until right then. His square jaw was set firmly as he waited for her to answer. Julia swallowed against her suddenly dry throat. "I... I spoke with Emily yesterday. She was upset. I should have made her stay with me. I knew something was going to happen."

"What did you talk about?" The sheriff's questions were businesslike, devoid of emotion.

"Um... she was worried something was going on with her husband. He seemed so angry, but I never thought he'd hurt her, not like this." Julia kept the details of the conversation to herself. It felt wrong to break her confidence, especially now.

"He didn't."

"If I'd... wait... what?" Julia shook her head, confused as she saw Emily walk out of the house with deputy Sam as escort. "Emily! She's... I don't understand."

"She's fine, but Thomas Peterson is dead."

## ~ Chapter 5 ~

Sitting alone in a small room, Julia knotted her fingers together. It was fidget or risk biting the nails down to the quick. Sheriff Barrett had asked her to come down to the station to talk about what happened. He assured her it was routine and told her not to be nervous, but she couldn't help feeling like a criminal as she hitched a ride in the back of the late-model interceptor sedan.

She had been led to a stark interview room, furnished with only a table and a couple metal chairs. There was an eyebolt in the center of the table—surely used for interrogating cuffed and dangerous suspects— that kept catching her eye. Julia tried looking away, but there was only the drab grayish paint that didn't invite anything but more nerves. The only other place to land her gaze was the rectangular one-way glass; that component of the room made her the most anxious of all, as she felt nothing short of a thousand unseen eyes boring into her, so she settled on watching her fidgeting fingers.

Julia's head jerked up when the door opened, and Sheriff Barrett strolled through carrying an official-looking folder; his muscular six-foot frame seemed to fill the doorway. "Sorry for the delay. Did anyone bring you something to drink? Coffee? Water?"

"It's all right; I'm fine. I'd really rather just get this over with. I mean, I don't know how I can help, but I'm willing to try." Julia's edginess was causing her to ramble.

Sheriff Barrett's expression softened, and the attractive smile he offered melted Julia's nerves. "I can understand that. This isn't exactly the most fun place to be."

"Is Emily all right?" Julia had been dying to ask since she locked eyes with the distraught woman being ushered into a different interview room.

"Don't worry about Mrs. Peterson—she's being taken care of. Right now, I want to focus on you and the ways *you* can help our investigation." He eased into the chair opposite Julia and placed the folder in front of him.

Julia tried unsuccessfully to still her restless fingers. Sheriff Jack Barrett wasn't a stranger to her; in fact, he'd been quite the familiar face around town. He'd stopped by Past Imperfect once or twice to say hello, and she'd often spotted him taking a coffee break at Blue Water Cafe. He'd always been a fixture of comfort in her mind—at least up until then, when his brawny frame felt more intimidating than reassuring.

Opening the folder, the sheriff looked down, then closed it as if changing his mind suddenly. "Why don't we start with why you were at the Peterson house this morning?" he questioned in a businesslike tone.

Julia tilted her head, confused. "I told you, I was worried about Emily. We had plans this morning and she didn't show up—didn't even respond to my text."

Deep in thought, Sheriff Barrett rubbed a large hand over the scruff along his jaw. Before he spoke, he leaned in over the table, rounding his shoulders towards Julia in a confiding manner. "I can appreciate that you seem awfully worried about your friend. Did something happen recently to give you extra cause for concern?" His question was direct, but there was an unexpected note of sympathy in his tone.

Julia was at a loss for words. She wanted to be honest but didn't want to risk causing any trouble for Emily. If she told the sheriff about the couple's marital problems and Tom's angry outburst, would it make

Emily seem guilty? She didn't want to give him fuel to make a case against her. Glancing up, she found his piercing eyes studying her. Warmth crept up her neck under his intense gaze. There was no more time for debating. "Emily and I spoke yesterday. She was upset. I was worried about her and asked her to stop by the shop this morning. When she didn't show up, I walked over to check on her." Julia rushed the words out.

The sheriff's eyes narrowed. "What made her upset in the first place?"

Julia's brow furrowed. She didn't want to tell him details about their conversation. Since she hadn't been at the scene, Julia couldn't be sure exactly what had happened, but knew in her gut that if her friend had harmed Thomas Peterson, it would have been an act of self-defense. There was no way Emily could kill someone in cold blood.

*We all are.*

Julia had been looking down at the table, not wanting to be caught in his gaze, but now her eyes darted around the cramped room, searching for the source of the comment. "Who was that?" she asked, peering over the sheriff's shoulder at her reflection in the two-way mirror. "Is someone listening in?"

Jack Barrett glanced over his shoulder and then back at Julia with a baffled expression playing over his sculpted features. "Mrs. Crawford?" The sheriff's voice was strained. "I need you to focus and tell me why it was that at the scene, you thought Emily was the one hurt?"

"Call me Julia, please." It might have seemed a trivial thing at such a time, but the sound of her formal name put an unfriendly distance between them, and she was in desperate need of a friend. "Mrs. Crawford is my ex-mother-in-law." Julia thought she saw the corners of his mouth twitch upward, but she couldn't read the emotion. Humor? Annoyance? "Before I answer, I want you to understand that I don't believe Emily has done anything wrong." Julia surprised herself with the firmness of her tone.

"Duly noted," the sheriff acknowledged, winding his hand in the air in a gesture that urged her to get on with it.

"Emily and Tom were having some problems," Julia said with a sigh. She felt like a traitor as she went on, "She found evidence that he was having an affair and meant to confront him last night. When I didn't hear from her this morning, I panicked, thinking something terrible must have happened... and it did."

"What time did you leave your home this morning?" the sheriff asked, making notes on a legal pad.

"I'm not sure." Julia felt flustered. "Oh, um, it must have been just a little while after I texted her. If you will give me back my bag, I can check my phone."

"Don't worry about that right now. We can verify the time later."

"What happened, anyway? How did Mr. Peterson die?" Julia tried to shift the tone of the conversation.

"That's what we're trying to figure out. We're still piecing it together."

Julia leaned forward, "What did Emily say happened?" Her curiosity took control, and she was helpless to cork the question.

The sheriff crossed his arms and gave her a sly smile. "Now, you know I can't tell you that."

Julia's lips pursed as she sat back. "Please... I've been honest with you, so what can you tell me? As a friend?"

The sheriff relaxed his arms on the table, lacing his fingers together. Julia took note of the wide silver band on his ring finger, and a twinge of sorrow pierced her heart. Though she'd never met Anne—she died two years before Julia moved to Grand Marais—it was obvious Jack still loved her. Julia heard through the gossip of the coffee klatch about how Jack sat at Anne's bedside day and night, staying with her until the end. Julia wished she'd met someone like Jack Barrett when she was younger. She couldn't imagine Graham wearing his ring to her funeral, let alone for years beyond her death.

Julia struggled with her emotions, unable to deny that she found the sheriff quite attractive but smart enough to realize she wasn't in a place to have coffee with him, let alone mount a serious effort to compete with his dead wife.

Sheriff Barrett ignored her question, posing another of his own. "Did you have reason to think Emily was in danger physically?"

Julia's fingers knotted again under the table. "I'm not sure. She told me no, but he did grab her. There was a small bruise on her arm."

A quick rap on the door sent her heart through her chest.

The door opened, and Sam, the deputy from last night, stepped in. "Excuse me." Sheriff Barrett rose, facing away from Julia. He kept his voice low so she couldn't overhear, and even though she craned her neck a bit to see what going on, there was no viewing anything beyond his broad back.

Julia gave up and slumped down in her chair. The nail of her ring finger suffered the brunt of her frustration. She forced her hand away from her mouth when the sheriff clicked the door closed, a new folder in hand. "Turns out there is something you might be able to help me with." He reclaimed his chair.

Julia perked up eagerly. "Sure, anything."

Opening the folder, he slid a photograph towards her. "What can you tell me about this?"

Julia's eyes widened as she looked at the photograph. She found herself staring at a picture of a familiar silver antique letter opener with repoussé scrollwork and a pierced lattice end surrounded by floral motifs. "I don't understand. Why do you have a picture of my letter opener?"

"Then you recognize it?"

"Of course, it's the letter opener I received with yesterday's shipment. How did you get a picture of it?" Butterflies fluttered in her stomach as she got the drift of where the conversation was headed.

"When did you have it in your possession last?" The sheriff ignored Julia's question.

"In the shop yesterday. I saw it there, so please tell me how you came to have a picture of it!" Julia pushed her fear down, but it crept into her voice anyway.

"It was discovered this morning." The sheriff's hands were flat on the table, one on either side of the picture.

"Wait, discovered? *Where*?" Julia fingered the photograph nervously.

*You know…*

Julia's eyes flicked from the table to the two-way glass as her chest tightened and her throat felt closed off. Where were the whispers coming from? Heat rose in her chest and perspiration formed on the back of her hairline. When her eyes landed back on the photograph, a wave of nausea went through her and she realized she wanted to look anywhere else but there. As her eyes fell on the wall behind the sheriff's right shoulder, the drab gray paint faded into a tall window covered in heavy drapes. They were so real, she could have walked over and pulled them open. When a rush of vertigo scrambled her senses, she squeezed her eyes shut, willing the voice and image to go away. *What's happening to me?*

"Mrs. Crawford? Are you all right?" Sheriff Barrett's voice sounded muffled, far away and underwater.

Something soft brushed Julia's hand, and her eyes flew open in fear. The drapery was gone, and the wall was bare and gray again. She took a deep breath in an attempt to settle herself. She looked at the sheriff, surprised to find his fingers pulling back from her hand and concern in his expression. "Y-yes, just tired. I didn't sleep well last night. I'm sorry, where did you say you found it?"

"Sticking out of Thomas Peterson's chest."

# Broken Promises

# ~ Chapter 6 ~

Julia turned the key in the lock and stepped inside her shop. Sheriff Barrett followed closely behind her. "I don't understand how it could have been used to kill Tom Peterson. It must be a copy or something," Julia offered, desperate for answers herself. She was certain the letter opener was in the desk drawer where she'd left it the previous afternoon. Snaking their way to the back of the shop, the two stopped at the desk. "A box arrived yesterday, and the letter opener was inside. I spent the afternoon working on its provenance, but I didn't have an opportunity to finish. I haven't looked at it since. It's not even in the inventory yet." Julia knew she was rambling but couldn't bear suffering the deafening silence of his gaze. She stooped down and yanked the large bottom drawer open, pulling out the wooden box. Breathing a sigh of relief, she handed the box to the sheriff. "Here, just like I said."

Jack Barrett opened the box, frowning as he turned his attention to Julia. "It's empty."

"What? That's not possible." Julia jumped up, startled, and a bit too quickly. Her hand fell against his firm upper arm to steady herself. At the horrible sight of the empty box, she was glad he was there. Her knees weakened and her chest felt tight again. Just the thought of someone using it to kill was more than she could take at that moment. She felt Jack's strong arm slide protectively around her, easing her into the chair.

"So, you don't know what happened to it?" he asked with mixture of disbelief and surprise in his voice.

Julia leaned forward, burying her face in her hands. "No; I told you. I put it in the desk, went to lunch, ran a few errands before coming back to the shop. I pulled it from the desk to examine it more closely, but…"

"But what?"

Julia hesitated, then realized she only made herself and Emily look guilty. "Emily stopped by the shop. I put it in the drawer, and we went upstairs to have a cup of tea and talk." Until that moment, Julia hadn't thought about Emily seeing where the letter opener was kept. *Could she have stolen it to use against her husband?* The theory sounded wild, but what else could make sense? Perhaps her friend was much more afraid than she'd let on. *Why use the letter opener? Unless she was hoping to have the shop under suspicion.* That thought chilled her.

"You're saying Emily Peterson was here when the weapon was out?"

"The letter opener," Julia corrected, "but yes. Lucy was here as well, and I'd imagine even some customers might have passed by when it was in view."

"Lucy Wells?" he asked in that small-town knowing tone.

Julia sighed; she was still getting used to the "everybody knows everybody" atmosphere. "Yes, she works in the shop a few days a week. I can call her if you'd like."

The sheriff made a note on his pocket pad. "Don't worry about that now. I'll contact her if I need to."

Julia noticed during their conversation that Jack's eyes furtively took in his surroundings. When he spoke, he looked directly at her, but otherwise his eyes scanned the shop. "It must have been stolen during the break-in." Julia mumbled the only conclusion she could come up with.

"The nine-one-one call you made last night?"

"Yes, I heard a noise from the shop last night. I felt stupid after I called when your deputy found my cat near an overturned lamp and everything else seemed to be in place. Sam took a report and ensured the doors were locked before he left. It seemed like a harmless false alarm, but maybe someone did break in after all." Julia felt her stomach lurch at the idea that there was an intruder in her shop, so close to where she was sleeping. She'd convinced herself that Henry was the cause of the noise, and this new revelation caused her fingers to tremble up to her mouth.

Jack stooped down, gently easing her hand away from her face. "It's all right. I'll check the report and have the patrol drive by the shop to look in on things tonight." Jack's soft tone eased Julia's fear. She looked at him, thinking she could happily lose herself in his smile. His fingers lingered on hers for a moment before he abruptly pulled them away and stood upright. "I'll check into things and let you know. For the time being, don't leave town." Jack's tone was all business again, shedding any residue of his unofficial behavior.

Julia nodded, still feeling the unexpected softness of his touch. Looking up, she found Jack watching her with an incomprehensible expression in his handsome features. *Is he thinking of the touch too? Or is he trying to decide whether I'm capable of murder?* Silence fell between them, broken by the shrill ring from his phone.

Snatching the smartphone from his belt clip, he answered: "This is Barrett… yeah… okay, yeah, be right there." Swiping the screen, he repositioned the phone in its holster. "I need to go," he announced abruptly, "but I'm going to have forensics stop by and process your place. So, don't touch anything else. There could be evidence as to who else may have been in that drawer."

Julia nodded again as she stood. She walked to the front of the shop with the sheriff. "They'll be by in a few hours after they finish up with the Peterson scene. I'll give you a call so you can open the door for them."

"Thank you for that. I'll stay close by." Julia closed and locked the door behind him, resting her forehead against the aged wooden door frame. The last 24 hours whirled in her head, leaving her confused and more than a little scared.

An hour later, Julia paced a track in her apartment floor. "This has to stop." She was going to go crazy if she wasn't there already. She grabbed her bag and headed out towards Artists' Point. The sun was warm, and there was just enough breeze to make the pines sway gently. She climbed onto the large, flat rocks and pulled out her sketch pad.

Julia grew up loving to draw. Aunt Sadie was the first person to support her desire to sketch. Julia's mother was more matter-of-fact about life and thought it a silly passing hobby. The sisters weren't close, partially because Sadie was at the Sorbonne by the time Julia's mother was born. Sadie had given Julia her first art set and sketch pad as a birthday present. From that moment, she sketched anything and everything she could. When it came time to decide between art and art history, she chose the former. Neither choice made her mother happy, and when Graham worked to convince Julia that art would never be a viable career, her mother was all too happy to take his side in the matter. At least with art history, she could work in a museum or gallery. Over their years together, she sketched less and less until her muse drained away. It was only after coming to Grand Marais that she rediscovered her first love. Sitting on the rocks near Artists' Point, she laid herself bare to the raw power of nature, watching waves crash over the edge of rock that created the outcropping and drawing out her inspiration once more. Julia sketched away the past sitting on those rocks, and in the process found herself. Now she hoped she could let go of the bizarre day she had experienced and gain some inner peace.

Julia used soft graphite to outline the large, flat, reddish stones, the crashing surf, and the dense pine trees inhabiting Artists' Point. Julia even sketched another artist into her drawing who was taking advantage of the same view. She captured the first hints of sunset before packing up and walking back to town. She wasn't ready to be alone in the shop, so she continued past it and turned left onto Wisconsin Avenue. Julia crossed the street and headed to the Gunflint Tavern. She just wanted a quiet dinner before heading home and couldn't face going back to the café that was surely buzzing with gossip by now.

As she crossed the next street, her phone rang. Not recognizing the phone number, she tapped the answer button with trepidation. "Hello? Yes, this she. Of course, I'll meet you there." Dropping the phone back into her bag, she said to herself, "Wasn't really hungry anyway." She was a bit disappointed to hear the female voice and not Jack Barrett's telling her the forensic team was on the way to her shop. She made a U-turn and arrived just as the boxy evidence collection truck pulled up.

Julia unlocked the front doors and switched on the lights, letting a young female tech enter first.

"Thanks. I'll need to get your fingerprints so we can exclude them." The smooth-faced investigator looked like she had just graduated from high school. She opened her kit, pulling out a digital fingerprinting device. She carefully collected an image of each of Julia's fingers on the pad in succession. Julia watched, fascinated at the images representing something uniquely her. When she finished, the tech said with a cheery smile, "Thank you; now, I need to process the scene. If you would kindly step out."

"What about Lucy's fingerprints? I'm sure they'll show up in your examination."

"We'll be sure to collect her prints as well." The investigator smiled again and started her work.

"I'll be upstairs if you need me." Julia left the tech to her work, though she couldn't get rid of a nagging feeling of dread as she headed to her apartment.

Julia sat in the Adirondack chair on the small deck above the shop. *Why would anyone steal an antique letter opener to murder someone?* she pondered. *Surely there were far better options, much easier to obtain, that would get the job done. Any kitchen knife would have worked. Unless they wanted me to be a suspect.* That thought clung hard, she thought she'd found home, but now she wasn't sure. Julia glanced up when King Henry strolled over the adjoining roof to rub against her leg. She got up and scooped the orange tabby into her arms, carrying him into the kitchen for his dinner. The roguish male enjoyed his feast, listening to Julia talk about everything that had happened. "It's just so strange. First, this beautiful letter opener shows up intended for Aunt Sadie, but it ends up being used to kill Tom Peterson." Finishing off her glass of wine, Julia remembered the note she had found in the box. Heading into the bedroom, she searched the dresser and nightstand for the piece of paper but couldn't find it. *Where did I put it?* Collapsing onto the bed in frustration, she glanced at the hamper, remembering she'd stashed it in her skirt pocket. Digging through the week's laundry, she found the skirt with the note still tucked safely inside. Unfolding the parchment, Julia discovered from the personalized stationery that it was from a woman named Charlotte Talbot.

*My Dearest Sarah,*

*It has been far too long since last we visited. I miss hearing your wonderful laughter and stories. I came across this unique piece at an estate sale while visiting London and thought you might be interested in it. I was told it has a fascinating history. I'm sure you'll have it in that wonderful book of knowledge. Don't let too much time pass before we can catch up.*

*Remembering Paris at midnight.*

*Love,*

*Charlotte*

The note explained who sent it, but the clue seemed useless. *Book of knowledge?* Julia fell back onto the bed, rereading the note. It was obvious the women were close. "They must have met while Aunt Sadie was in Paris at the Sorbonne." She sighed softly. "I should let her know about Sadie's passing." Curling up on her side, Julia felt her reclaimed life slipping away.

Anne Willow

## ~ Chapter 7 ~

"Have a safe drive back to the Cities." Julia handed her only customer of the morning a purchase receipt. Once the carved oak side table with the delicate claw feet was safely in the customer's car, Julia forced a friendly wave and headed back into the shop. She looked around, deciding whether to close Past Imperfect for lunch while things were quiet. She was worried about Emily and exhausted from another fitful night's sleep and the work of cleaning off the investigative powder coating every surface of her shop.

Julia kept rehashing it all in her mind. She knew Emily had been upset with her husband, but enough to kill him? "Maybe it was an accident." *But if it wasn't premeditated, why take the letter opener? Emily was no thief or kleptomaniac. If she had taken the letter opener, surely there was a good reason behind it. Unless...?* Julia sat up straight in her desk chair. The new thought was so ludicrous, she couldn't believe it had crossed her mind. *Had someone used the letter opener to frame her specifically?* Julia glanced at the picture of Aunt Sadie perched just beyond her blotter. Picking it up, she said, "I wish you could tell me what happened." Sighing, she replaced the picture. "Well, don't feel bad, Henry wasn't much help either. Why would someone want to use *my* antique letter opener to kill Emily's husband?"

"Kill whose husband?"

Julia jumped, her hand flying up to her chest. "Lucy, I didn't hear you come in."

"Didn't mean to startle you, but what about a murder weapon?" Lucy dropped her backpack and sat in the chair nearest Julia's desk. "What's going on? Does it have something to do with all the police cars I saw yesterday?"

"Yes—Tom Peterson was murdered yesterday." Julia wasn't sure how much to tell her. She was still young. Julia watched Lucy's reaction, also surprised that she hadn't been contacted by the police.

"What happened?" Lucy asked, her tone flat.

Surprised at the lack of emotional response, Julia dismissed it as shock. "He was stabbed in his home. Do you remember seeing that new letter opener after I showed it to you?" Julia asked, a glint of hope in her voice.

Lucy furrowed her brow. "Yeah, the one you put in the wooden box? I saw you slip it in the desk drawer right before you went upstairs with Mrs. Peterson. Why are you asking about it?"

"Think. It's important. Are you sure you didn't move it?" Julia tried to keep her tone calm.

Lucy shifted in her chair. "Of course, I didn't move it. I wouldn't go into your desk without asking you first," she lashed out, hurt evident in her tone.

Julia reached over, collecting Lucy's hands. "I'm sorry, sweetie. I wasn't accusing you, just trying to figure things out."

Lucy squeezed Julia's fingers with her usual happy smile. "It's okay—but tell me what's going on. What does the letter opener have to do with Mr. Peterson dying?"

Julia told Lucy about stopping by the Petersons' only to find out that someone had stabbed Tom with the antique letter opener. "Actually, I saw you on my walk over, but you must have been lost in thought. You didn't seem to hear me."

The corners of Lucy's lightly tinted mouth dropped. "I... I spent the morning at the library. You know I have classes starting up soon and wanted to get a head start. I'm sorry, you must think me a terrible person for not seeing you."

Julia captured Lucy's hands in her own. The young woman looked like she was going to cry, refusing to meet Julia's eyes. "Honey don't worry about it. Are you sure you're okay?"

Lucy sighed. "I'll be okay. Just had a fight with my mom is all. She went out the other night with her new boyfriend. When she came home, she was twisted up over something. I asked what was wrong, and she just snapped at me."

"People get into arguments. It isn't your fault. I'm sure your mom wasn't upset with you." Julia tried to reassure Lucy.

"Yeah, I know. It's like you and your husband."

Julia's brow furrowed. "I'm sorry?"

Lucy blushed. "I'm sorry. I didn't mean to say something out of turn."

"It's okay. What were you talking about, though?"

"You know it's a small town. Everybody knows everybody."

Julia understood how gossip could spread rapidly in a small town, but she didn't like being the subject of conversation. "Lucy, tell me—what have you heard?"

"You told me the shop belonged to your aunt. You have a light spot on your ring finger and whenever your phone plays a particular song, you tense up," Lucy offered.

"I'm confused. What does that have to do with what I told you about Tom Peterson?"

"My mother says a woman who can't keep her husband happy is risking him finding another."

Julia's stomach tightened, and tears stung the back of her eyes. Shooting out of the chair, Julia turned her back to Lucy. "Your mother thinks I couldn't keep my husband happy?" Her voice broke with embarrassed anger. "She should mind her own business." She stalked upstairs. Once at the top, she closed and locked the door, falling back against it and sliding to the floor. "Maybe she's right. Was it my fault?" Wrapping her arms around her knees, Julia allowed herself to sob uncontrollably. As the tears fell, she realized the guilt she was feeling wasn't just about Graham and her lost marriage. It was about the murder and someone using something that had belonged to *her* to carry it out. She hadn't felt like herself since that letter opener had arrived.

Julia suddenly felt dizzy, even from the floor; the room was wobbling while colors shifted. She saw the dark silhouette of a man looming before her.

"Hello?" she called out in fear, her voice barely audible.

But then the shadow seemed to slump over, and when Julia glanced down at her hands, they were dripping with blood.

"*No!*" she shouted, squeezing her eyes shut. When she dared to open them again, several minutes later, her apartment was still, looking just as it should.

"What's happening to me?" Julia asked aloud, and just as she said it, a thought that was too horrible to be true struck her. Where these visions she was having some kind of memories? Could the shadowy man have been Tom Peterson? She didn't feel like a murderer, but why would anyone else besides her have used the letter opener? None of it made any sense.

An hour later, her tears spent, and her balance regained, Julia collected herself and headed back downstairs. The shop was quiet. "Lucy?" Not getting an answer, Julia exhaled. *Why should she stay, after the way you ran out?* Julia pressed the heel of her hand to her temple, willing the internal voice away. At the bottom of the stairs, Julia heard a sniffle from the back of the store. Heading towards it, she said softly, "Lucy?"

Lucy was sitting just as Julia had been—her knees drawn up, her face buried in her arm. Julia closed the distance between them, stooping down. "Lucy. It's all right."

Lucy looked up, her tear-stained face full of apology. She threw her arms around Julia's neck. "I'm so sorry to upset you like that. I would die before I hurt you." The words tumbled out in a jerking motion, as if they were being strangled by withheld sobs.

Julia pulled back. "Shhh... it's all right. I shouldn't have run off. You just hit a raw nerve, that's all. It's not your fault. You didn't know." Slipping her hand into her skirt pocket, Julia offered Lucy her embroidered linen handkerchief.

Lucy wiped her eyes and nose. "I don't think like my mom does. I was only repeating what she said. I think any man who cheats is a jerk."

Julia couldn't help but snort a chuckle at her lack of swearing. Lucy was sweet. Julia never heard her use foul language; it was one of the things she liked about Lucy. "Look at the two of us, with our matching red and puffy eyes. Come on, why don't we close for the day and get lunch? My treat. I think both of us could use the fresh air."

Lucy smiled, took the offered hand, and stood. She grabbed her pink backpack and joined Julia at the door. Julia turned the wooden plaque she'd painted with *Open* on one side and *Closed* on the other. She made sure to lock the shop before the two headed towards the busier part of town.

# Broken Promises

## ~ Chapter 8 ~

The café was busier than normal, especially so late in the afternoon. The couple occupying Julia's favorite booth didn't look as if they were leaving anytime soon. "Looks like we're sitting at the counter." They found two stools and settled in.

Lucy leaned over. "Why's it so busy?"

Julia shook her head. "Curiosity for other people's troubles." The gawkers reminded Julia of those onlookers passing the scene of a tragic accident. The ability for people to find pleasure in another person's unhappiness still surprised her.

Carol came over, a little breathless. "Sorry for the wait. Business is hopping."

"We can see that." Julia had hoped to see Sandy so she could ask after Emily. It bothered her that she still hadn't had a chance to speak with her. "It makes sense, with Emily out."

"Out? She's in back. They called me in when the crowd poured in. I don't mind the extra hours, but with everything that's happened, you'd think she'd take time off." Carol shrugged and smiled tightly. "Now, what can I get for you ladies?"

Julia wasn't ready to think about food. Lowering her voice, she asked, "How is she?"

Carol glanced up from her pad. "She's all right, considering, but..." the waitress seemed to debate internally before adding, "in a way, you might say she's better off."

Julia noticed Lucy duck behind the menu at the mention of Emily. She hoped the conversation wasn't upsetting her, but she couldn't stop there. "What do you mean? Better off how?"

Carol leaned closer, resting on her elbows. "With that husband of hers out of the picture, she can finally be happy and find someone who really loves her."

Julia's brow knitted. "Why do you think she was so unhappy?" *Did everyone know about Tom's affair?*

"We've all seen the two of them argue; it was a common occurrence around here. Then the same day or maybe the next, he'd show up with flowers and sweet talk." Carol rolled her eyes. "I tried to convince her it was all for show, but she wouldn't listen."

"What did they argue about?" Julia's mother would have scolded her for gossiping, but that never stopped her mother from talking about the neighbors.

"He was a good-looking guy with a killer smile. It's easy to see he would have turned heads. One afternoon about a week or so ago, I saw them at the boat launch at the top of the Gunflint. I figured they were going into the boundary waters for the day, but when Emily climbed out of Tom's truck," she lowered her voice conspiratorially, "I realized it *wasn't* Emily."

"Who was it?" Julia urged her on.

"I don't know. No one I've seen come in here, but she was a young, pretty thing with long blonde hair. Wore it back in a ponytail. She was all about him. It looked mutual."

"I see." The feeling of being watched crept up her back. Julia glanced around to find several diners staring at her and whispering. Uncomfortable, she shifted in her seat, and focused on Carol. "Do you think she killed him?"

"Emily? Maybe, though I heard the sheriff is looking at someone else. Don't know who, but I'm sure they'll get things figured out soon."

"I hope so." A young man sitting at the counter to Julia's left interjected. "Sorry, didn't mean to eavesdrop, but with the music festival starting, we don't need some crazy murderer running loose."

Carol grabbed a pot of coffee and refilled his cup. "I'm sure they'll solve it soon and the festival will be a hit. Then again, we shouldn't complain—look what it's doing for business!"

Sipping from the hot cup, he replied, "True, but if they don't solve it soon, people may stay away out of fear."

A group seated at the table in the corner called her. "Sorry, be right back." She rushed away before Julia could say another word.

Lucy leaned over towards Julia again to cut out eavesdroppers. "Do you think it was someone he knew or some crazy person? I mean, I've never been afraid to walk around here at night, but now I don't know."

Sliding her arm around Lucy's shoulder, Julia pulled her into a hug. "I don't think there's a crazy person running around killing people." And then her stomach dropped as a buzzing sound filled her ears, drowning out the clamor of the cafe. *How sure are you? Maybe you're the one that's crazy.*

Emily appeared on the other side of the counter, her appearance jarring Julia from her morbid thoughts. "So, what can I get for you ladies?" Her voice was hoarse and forced.

Julia looked up, mystified as to how the woman had the strength to be at work after everything she'd gone through in the short span of time. Her heart broke seeing that the circles under Emily's bloodshot eyes had darkened, but she tried to play it off, not wanting to embarrass Emily in front of Lucy. "The usual and whatever Lucy wants." She forced her tone to stay relaxed.

Emily jotted down Julia's order then looked in Lucy's direction. "What would you like?"

"A cheeseburger, fries, and a cola." Lucy swung her legs a bit at the bar stool, making her appear even younger than her 18 years. Julia was glad to see that her usual happy smile had replaced the emotional downpour from earlier, but it was odd that nothing in her expression suggested she even noticed Emily's haggard appearance.

Julia watched the exchange between the two of them, thinking that maybe they were both were a bit off. How could Lucy not react to Emily standing there, looking exhausted and shattered… and how could Emily be holding it together so well, feigning cheerfulness as she asked for their orders? Nothing made sense.

"I'll come right back with your drinks." Emily walked off, disappearing into the kitchen.

Julia nodded absentmindedly. Everything felt a bit surreal, the hubbub and clinking of cutlery merging into a woozy torrent of sound. What she wouldn't give for a few minutes alone with Emily to sort things out and find some answers. "Here you go." Sandy appeared, porcelain teapot in hand. It was obvious every waitress was on hand to deal with the crowd. She placed it on the counter with the matching cup and saucer, then gave Lucy her cola and a straw. "Em put your order in; she needed to take a break. It's been a busy day, not to mention she isn't exactly herself. I'm glad Carol could come in and help."

Julia followed Emily with her eyes, watching where she disappeared into a small vestibule that branched off towards the kitchen and restrooms. "Would you excuse me? I'm going to wash my hands before we eat." Not waiting for a response, Julia slipped off the stool and headed to the ladies' room. The swinging door opened to a tiled room with two stalls. Julia could see a pair of urban hikers peeking from below the smaller stall.

"Emily? It's Julia." Her voice echoed against the subway tile, and she could hear sniffling from behind the door. "Can we talk?"

"I'm all right," Emily protested as she whimpered.

"Emily. Please open the door," Julia whispered, not hiding her concern. She was just about to give up hope when the door opened a bit.

Emily's eyes were red with renewed crying, her nose blushed with the constant wiping and sniffling. "I'm sorry. Seems every time you see me, I'm blubbering like an idiot."

Julia smiled sympathetically. "Don't worry about that." Not knowing what else to do, Julia spread her arms out hesitantly, leaning towards the other woman.

Emily surprised Julia when she fell gratefully into the offered embrace. Julia held Emily tightly while she cried, feeling her desperate cling while her face was buried in the hollow of her shoulder. Neither woman spoke for several minutes. Eventually, Emily pulled back and pulled the linen handkerchief Julia gave her from her pocket to wipe at her eyes.

Julia sighed and gave Emily what she hoped was an encouraging smile. "I am so sorry for everything that's happened," she said. "This must be a nightmare for you."

"You have nothing to be sorry for." Emily's voice was shaky, perhaps from the crying, although Julia felt there might be more to it. *Fear*, perhaps. "You helped me far more than I could have asked for, but I never thought you'd do *that*," Emily blurted out.

Julia tried to piece together what Emily was saying, her brain wrapped in foggy confusion. "I haven't done much at all—just trying to be a friend."

"A friend? Is that what you call it? How many friends can you say would do what you did? I mean, I was angry at first, but then I realized what you'd really done for me." Emily moved to the sink and splashed water on her face. "I never would have escaped him without you. I couldn't even admit to myself—let alone anyone else—how he was hurting me."

Julia's confusion deepened. "Wait, what are you talking about? Do you think I had something to do with Tom's murder?"

Emily stepped back over to Julia as she dried her hands, the brown paper crunching under her frenzied hand movements. "We don't have to talk about it anymore. I'm not trying to get you in trouble for this, but you'd better be glad I had a solid alibi; otherwise, I could have gone down for your crime! Why did you use something from your shop? Not the best idea." Grasping Julia's arms, Emily looked deep into her eyes and assured her, "But don't worry—I when the sheriff questioned me, I didn't tell them anything of our conversation. I wasn't going to give them motive. He asked me about you, and I told him there was no way you could have done anything like that. We'll keep the secret between us." Emily pulled Julia into another hug and then released her abruptly. "I don't want to talk about it or think about it ever again. I know you thought you were doing what needed to be done and everything... I don't know... I need to get back to work."

Julia's brows knitted together tightly. "Emily, wait. I have nothing to hide—"

Emily interrupted her from the doorway. "I get it..." Emily made a show of zipping her lips and tossing away the imaginary key. Then, without another word, she left the restroom.

Julia leaned back against the blue-and-white-tiled wall, almost knocking over the decorative fern in the corner. Her stomach twisted as the room tilted. Chaotic thoughts vortexed threatened to put Julia on the floor. It was bad enough that the sheriff might suspect Julia of the murder and worse that Emily seemed to believe wholeheartedly in her guilt. But the worst thing of all was that Julia herself didn't know what to believe. Never had she experienced visions or hallucinations, or anything that would have made her question her sanity. But suddenly she wondered, *Did I kill Tom Peterson?* She remembered falling asleep in the chair that night. Was it possible she went into a sort of fugue state and committed the murder when she was out of sorts? Her trembling hand flew up and covered her mouth. Julia shook her head, "Wait, why would I report a robbery if I did it?" A glimmer of hope kindled.

*Alibi…*

The persistent voice argued. "Great, now even I don't believe me."

If Sheriff Barrett harbored similar doubts about Julia, then she might be looking at her reclaimed life through metal bars.

# Broken Promises

## ~ Chapter 9 ~

Julia wasn't sure how much time had passed before she returned to the counter. It had taken her a good while to gather herself, and her BLT sandwich was waiting for her when she got back.

Lucy was already munching away happily on her burger. She stopped mid-bite and stared at Julia. "Are you all right? You look like you've seen a ghost."

Julia couldn't speak. She was disappointed that she hadn't collected herself enough before returning to her seat; her heart was still pounding in her throat. Picking up her teacup, Julia tried to cover her trembling hands. The nervous clinking of the china cup against the delicate saucer did little to hide the panic inside.

"Julia." Lucy reached over to still Julia's hand. "Tell me what's wrong."

Julia looked at Lucy, and for the first time, she didn't look like a teenager. Instead as if a switch had been flipped, there was deep attention in her gaze, and she seemed genuinely worried. "To be honest, I've lost my appetite." Pulling money from her bag, Julia placed it on the counter. "Why don't you have this boxed and take it home? I think I'll go back and close the shop for the rest of the day."

Emily was behind the counter again, filling a cup of coffee from a carafe. Even as the steaming liquid splashed into the mug, she didn't take her birdlike stare away from Julia. Unsettled and feeling as if her world was crumbling, Julia grabbed her bag and rushed out the door.

Julia headed out of the café and turned left instead of right. The road ended at Lake Superior Trading Post and Java Moose. Leaving the tar-paved road, Julia traversed the rock-clustered beach that surrounded the inlet. Anchored boats still in town from the fisherman's festival dotted the inlet and would for a few more weeks. Lake Superior was well-known for giving even the most experienced sailor unexpected weather, even in late summer.

Seeing several artists on the water break, Julia headed to Artists' Point. Staying along the far edge of the small wooded area, she dropped onto the flat red rocks and watched the water. The afternoon tide danced along the rocky border. Julia felt caught by the tide; she felt herself being pulled by the lake's demanding waters. What could she do? If Emily thought that she was capable of murdering Tom, then surely the sheriff thought she was guilty as well.

*It was **your** letter opener.*

Julia turned to respond but found herself quite alone. She was sure she heard someone speak but it must have been the whispering waters. The stress was causing her to crack, and a bubble of laughter fought its way up her throat. If Julia herself wasn't even sure what happened that night, how would she prove to anyone else that she was innocent? She tried to think of everyone who knew about the letter opener or had been there while it was out. Who else besides her had access?

There was Emily, first, but she claimed to have an alibi. Then there was Lucy, of course, but Julia shook her head. "Not possible. Lucy wouldn't hurt a soul, let alone stab a man to death. Besides, what reason would she have to kill him?" She thought some more. There could have been other people in the shop near the letter opener. It's not like she had locked it away, and she'd left Lucy to deal with customers on her own for a while the day before she noticed it was missing. Perhaps if there was a trial, Julia could convince the jury of reasonable doubt. All she had to do was convince herself first.

Everything she had worked for during the last two months ebbed away. Julia wanted to run, but where? *Back to Graham and the Cities?* "He'd love that," she spat bitterly.

"Who'd love what?"

The unexpected question startled Julia. Shifting, she lost her footing. A sure, strong hand stopped her from slipping into the water. "Thank you." Adjusting herself back further onto the stone seat, Julia looked up to find Sheriff Jack Barrett looking at her silently. She couldn't make out what he was thinking, but she had the overwhelming wish that he would pull her into his arms and tell her everything was a dream. His hand pulled away from the fire instead, dashing her hopes.

"You didn't answer my question." His voice floated through the air between them, both strong and caring, yet bound by professionalism.

"It wasn't anything; just talking to myself." Julia didn't lie, exactly, but talking about Graham with Jack Barrett was the last thing she wanted to do. "What brings you out here?" The false levity in her tone fell flat.

"May I?" Sheriff Barrett gestured to the space next to Julia. Her heart fluttered with renewed hope, pushing aside all her tormented thoughts of bloodguilt.

"Certainly."

Sheriff Barrett dropped easily next to her, keeping a respectable distance between them. "We need to talk."

"And you knew to find me out here?" Julia caught her lower lip, feeling flattered somehow. *Maybe he feels a connection?*

"Actually, I was just at your shop when I saw you cross from the inlet."

She tried not to let her disappointment show. "Oh. Makes sense." *Give it up, Juls. He thinks you killed a man; he's not going to ask you out for coffee.*

An awkward silence fell between them. Kelly Clarkson sang out, startling Julia. *Oh God, not now.* Shoving her hand into her bag, she searched for the phone to silence the ringer. "Since you've been gone…" blared the catchy pop song. Her face flushed a deep crimson. Julia's finger found the side button and flicked it; a blissful silence followed.

Sheriff Barrett broke it after a few beats. "It's about the Peterson case."

Julia's heart stopped beating again. She didn't want to think about the case or the letter opener—slick with fresh blood—ever again. She could only nod.

"The lab dusted the letter opener for fingerprints. Only one clear set came back."

Julia forced herself to breathe. *It's okay; they have fingerprints, and you'll be exonerated.* "That's good, isn't it?"

"Julia." He paused, looking at her with the oddest expression.

Julia loved how her name sounded when he said it, but the expression stole the pleasure. She realized he had only used her first name one other time, outside the Peterson murder scene.

He set his expression firm again. "You need to come with me, Mrs. Crawford." The sheriff stood and offered Julia a hand up.

Julia ignored his palm, fear squeezing her insides. "Wait, why?" There is it was again, the formal use of her last name. Hearing him add *Mrs.* only twisted the blade. He was no longer the handsome Jack, but all sheriff, and it sounded like he was arresting her.

"The only fingerprints found on the letter opener were yours."

# Broken Promises

## ~ Chapter 10 ~

"I don't understand why I'm here." Julia's fingers twisted into knots waiting for an answer. She was back in that horrible gray room. "It's not possible for my fingerprints to be on the letter opener; I never touched it other than when I had curator's gloves on. The oils from humans can damage antiques."

"So, you never touched any part of it?" The sheriff raised one eyebrow, staring her down with uncertainty.

This was the proof she had been waiting for, the evidence that she was a monster. It was only a matter of time before it came to light. Now there was no denying she killed Tom Peterson, since there was no other reason her prints should be on the letter opener.

Julia frowned, memory dawning on her. In all the chaos, she'd forgotten, but now she was remembering how she had knocked the box off the desk and reflexively picked up the letter opener bare-handed. "Wait, I did touch it." Unexpected embarrassment colored her cheeks, and she felt like a child inventing a story to avoid punishment. "I knocked it over and the box fell off the desk. I touched it when I was setting it right again. Later that afternoon I had it out, researching its provenance, but that's not out of the ordinary."

Sheriff Barrett sighed. "Mrs. Crawford…"

Julia had come to realize over the past few days that she didn't like the sheriff's business tone. She much preferred the softer, less accusing one. "I told you, I'm no longer Mrs. Crawford," she snapped. The words hung in the air, daggers of a shrew; she regretted them. "I… I'm sorry, I shouldn't have spoken to you like that." The sheriff's green eyes only stared, making Julia shift nervously. It frustrated her how this man could flutter her stomach in any situation.

"It's all right."

Julia wasn't sure whether she heard the softness back in his tone or if she just wished it was there, but she went on calmly this time, "I had the letter opener out, researching provenance later that day. Anyone who was in the shop had access to it just as easily as I did. I didn't keep my eye on it the whole day. And then there's the matter of the break-in." Julia didn't care if it was just Henry messing about; she was going to use every bit of ammunition she had to avoid implication in this mess. "At first, I thought it was my cat, but now I'm not so sure. Someone—*anyone*—could have taken the letter opener."

Sheriff Barrett only stared at her, his eyes thoughtful.

Forcing her fingers from their knots, Julia rested them on the table. "Please, how can I convince you that I didn't do this? I don't even know Tom Peterson, let alone have a reason to kill him." The little voice in Julia's head disagreed. *He was just like Graham. You had every reason to do it.*

Not surprisingly, the sheriff ignored her question and went on with his own. "What brought you to Grand Marais?"

Julia felt sick. *Why am I thinking such terrible thoughts?* She wished she'd left her fingers in their sailor's knots. "My aunt Sadie passed away. She left the shop to me."

Sheriff Barrett smiled. "I remember her. She was a fine lady and had a quick wit that could turn heads. I also remember she was a bit of a spitfire."

Julia didn't suppress the smile his comment brought about. "Yes, she could be a pistol. At least according to my mother." *Great, Julia. Bring up a gun when talking about murder.*

"Her niece seems very much like her."

Julia nodded absentmindedly, then realized he was referring to her. The warmth of a blush filled her cheeks.

Sheriff Barrett shifted in his seat. "Why didn't your husband accompany you?"

The comment was like a punch that threatened to send her to the floor. Tears stung her eyes as she swallowed, trying to keep her composure. Julia wasn't ready to talk to anyone in Grand Marais about Graham — especially not Jack Barrett. "We're separated," she whispered. It was all she could manage to tell him without crumbling completely.

"Why?" The professional tone gave way to his personal side. Julia wasn't sure if it was Jack or the sheriff asking, but she didn't think it was either one's business.

Taking a moment, Julia collected her thoughts, building a mental dam to bar her emotions. "Irreconcilable differences."

The sheriff's dark brows furrowed. "Ah."

"Not everyone has a perfect marriage!" The words lashed out before Julia could corral them within her flimsy barricade.

Sheriff Barrett sat back, his arms crossing over his chest. Julia watched the sting of her sharp tone shadow his face, fighting with the professional mantle that seemed to stiffen over his shoulders.

Julia buried her face in her hands. "I'm so sorry. I didn't mean to sound so sharp with you. It's just that—"

Sheriff Barrett reached across the table, lightly touching her wrist and stopping her mid-sentence. "I've been a sheriff in Grand Marais for twenty years. I was the youngest elected in the state. I'd like to think that by now I am a good judge of character." He tapped the folder on the table with a sudden grin. "Based on the evidence and my own observations, I believe you."

Julia's jaw dropped. "You do?" *You're going to get away with it after all.*

"You seem surprised." His face was a stage mask; Julia couldn't tell what he was thinking.

"Surprised doesn't seem to be a strong enough word." Internally, Julia wanted to throw her arms around him, feel him hold her, and ask him to make it all go away. *How can you trust him?* "I guess I was imagining that the whole town thought I was a murderer."

"The murder weapon belongs to you, so the prints can easily be expected. Then there's the matter of the suspected break-in. Some might say you staged it to make yourself appear innocent, but I listened to the nine-one-one call you made and questioned my deputy after the fact. Your fear that night sounded genuine to both me and Sam." The sheriff gave a mischievous smile before adding, "No offense, but I don't think you're that good of an actress. Your emotions play over your face as clear as written words."

Julia felt her neck grow hot, a mixture of relief and embarrassment tingling on the surface of her skin.

"My belief aside, though, the DA is going to look at what he has before him." Sheriff Barrett's voice had gone serious again, and he was flipping through the papers in the folder. "We've been butting heads on this one a bit, but I think I can…"

The door opened, and a young man in a grey tailored suit stepped into the room, an expensive leather briefcase in his hand. The newcomer was tall and lean and looked like he took care of his appearance. His manner of dress and posture belonged more in New York or Chicago than northern Minnesota. "Sheriff Barrett." He placed the black briefcase on the table without a word to Julia.

Sheriff Barrett nodded. "Julia Crawford, this is County Attorney Simon Tinsdale."

At the mention of his name, the young man with blond hair trained his eyes on her. "I take it you've been read your rights and have waived an attorney."

Julia stared at him in shock. "Wait... what?" Panic surged again; Julia's pounding heart momentarily drowned out all other sound.

Sheriff Barrett spoke quietly to Mr. Tinsdale, but Julia couldn't make out what he said over her heartbeat. Whatever it was, Mr. Tinsdale did not look happy. "You are questioning her without an attorney present or having read her rights?"

*No...no...this isn't happening.* Julia wrapped her arms around herself. She realized the attorney was speaking about her. "I'm sorry, what?"

"I understand you haven't been read your rights. My apologies; that should have happened before you were questioned. Do you have an attorney you'd like to call?" Mr. Tinsdale asked in a perturbed tone.

"I haven't done anything wrong," Julia protested. She looked to Jack for help, and a nearly imperceptible wink flicked over his right eye. Was he trying to tell her something?

"Of course," he said glibly. "Your fingerprints were found on the murder weapon. I think the evidence tells a different story," Mr. Tinsdale replied in a patronizing tone.

And then suddenly Julia understood. The lawyer was trying to scare her. He didn't have enough evidence for a conviction, so he wanted to spook her into confessing something. "I'm not a child; you don't need to use little words," Julia fired back at him. She saw the slightest nod from the sheriff, as if he were cheering her on, and it infused her with the courage she needed to keep going. "Yes, the letter opener came from my shop; it should have my fingerprints on it. Why wouldn't it?"

Mr. Tinsdale pursed his lips and glared down at Julia. She thought she could detect a slight tic in the corner of his eye. "Then, Mrs. Crawford, you'll understand how it looks."

"I understand how you *want* it to look, but as I've told you, it was mine and I touched it. Real, damning evidence would be if my fingerprints were found *at* the murder scene. How many of my prints have you found there?" Julia clung desperately to her courage.

The room fell silent. Julia glanced at the sheriff, who appeared almost proud as he waited for the county attorney to answer.

When he remained silent, Julia pressed on. "They wouldn't have been found anywhere else, since I've never been in the Peterson house. Why would I lack enough intelligence to leave fingerprints on the murder weapon but somehow be smart enough not to touch anything else? Does that make sense to you? Do you think it would make sense to a jury?"

Sheriff Barrett didn't speak; he only watched Julia as she fought for her freedom with a sudden outburst of vigor. His eyes teased a fleeting smile, but he managed to remain businesslike.

Clearing his throat, Mr. Tinsdale looked down his narrow nose, staring at her dismissively. "The investigation is ongoing. I suggest you engage an attorney's services." He closed his briefcase. "Sheriff Barrett, if you'll step out with me for a moment." He turned and walked out of the room, leaving the door open.

Sheriff Barrett sighed. He didn't make eye contact with Julia as he slid his chair back, left the room, and closed the door behind him.

Julia's stomach lurched when the door clicked shut. She wondered if her words meant anything at all. Was she fighting a losing battle? If she had plunged that letter opener into Tom Peterson's flesh, did she even deserve a defense? Resting her elbows on the table, she covered her face with trembling hands. The adrenaline rush that came from trying to prove her innocence to Mr. Tinsdale, the sheriff, and—most importantly—herself had left her withered and shaking.

# Broken Promises

~ Chapter 11 ~

Deputy Sam left Julia at her shop with a friendly nod. Although the sheriff had released her and she was off the hook for the moment, he had ordered her to remain in town until things were cleared up completely. After spending more than an hour in the grey, windowless room, the last place she wanted to be was indoors, alone with her idle mind. Pulling her bag onto her shoulder, she headed towards the rocky beach just past Artists' Point.

The stretch of public beach, a favorite agate-hunting ground for visitors, ran along the back patios of several local hotels. Julia was grateful to find it quiet, especially after sunset. Strolling along, listening to the water lap onto the rocks, she turned the last few days over in her head. She could hear the distant pounding of hammers as crews worked on preparations for the festival.

The familiar song that she had grown to despise by association rang out, disturbing her precious peace. Julia grabbed the phone from her bag, irritated. Seeing Graham's name displayed, Julia slid the icon to answer. *What a perfect ending to such a terrible day.* "Hi, Gra—"

"What the hell did you do, Juls?" Graham's anger cut her off. "I got served with divorce papers?"

*Obviously, he isn't going with the "beg to get me back" approach.* "Graham, we've been separated for two months. Don't you think it's time to stop living in limbo?" Julia dug for the courage she'd displayed with the district attorney but came up empty. Perhaps her well of moxie was finally depleted.

As if on cue, Graham's tone softened. "Limbo? I thought you needed time to settle your aunt's estate and then come home. It was never my understanding that your moving would be the end of us."

*Oh, how he loves to change the narrative to fit his point of view. He knows perfectly well why I left.* "Yes, I needed to take care of Aunt Sadie's estate, but I've been making a home here. This was the agreement and you knew that. This isn't some holiday; I've got friends here, and I've started to sketch again." Julia felt a strange buzzing in her ears, and the beautiful scenery seemed to fade in and out for just a second. She took a breath, focusing on the splash of the tide.

"Juls, sweetheart, it's been months. I miss you. You know you hate living alone and I hate being without you. Nothing says we can't go back and visit your friends every so often. It's only four hours away. You don't even have to sell the store... we'll work out the details. Come on, baby; I know we've had a rough patch, but being apart isn't fixing things. You belong with me."

There it was, the condescending, I'll-make-the-decisions-for-you tone Julia hated. It was how Graham got her to give up her opportunity for art school. Suddenly Julia realized that talking to this man made her feel trapped, and that she'd felt confined for all the years she was with him.

*You can't open the door. He won't let you.*

And then she could see a door in her mind: a heavy old thing with six panels and thick, dark molding. It barred her way as long as Graham was in her life. But it was more than a metaphor somehow. She could see nicks and scratch marks in the finish and even smell the oak wood. Even though it didn't make sense, some part of her knew this door quite well. "You'll never cage me again," Julia said into the phone harshly. "I won't let you."

"Cage you? Geez, Juls, you make me sound like a monster!"

Julia raised her voice. "You *are* a monster, and a lying one at that. You couldn't keep a promise to save your life."

"J-Juls!" Graham stammered to find his words. "What are you talking about? This doesn't even sound like you!"

Julia opened her mouth, poised for her next onslaught of words, when movement just past the Shoreline Motel near Drury Lane Books caught her attention. She could make out two unknown figures standing just far enough outside the illumination from the old-fashioned black lampposts that she couldn't make out their features. She could make out the tone of an argument, however, as one figure's arms flailed angrily.

Julia moved closer, carefully staying near the break wall. She watched as one figure pushed the other, the force causing the attacked shadow to skim the edges of the dim pool of light from the streetlamp. "Sandy?" Julia whispered, making out the curve of her heart-shaped face and the gleaming wisps of wavy hair. She tried to see who had pushed Sandy, but whoever it was stayed firmly planted in the shadows.

"Julia?" Graham's voice was startling, since Julia had forgotten her cell phone was pressed against her ear.

She whispered firmly, "I can't talk now," then disconnected the call and turned off her ringer, careful to keep the soft glow against her chest so it wouldn't be detected in the darkness. Julia ditched it into her bag and crept closer, making her way toward the chairs and firepit outside the bookstore. She hoped they would give her enough cover to not be noticed.

"Look, this is your fault, so don't threaten me." Sandy pushed back, her arms thrusting against the other figure. "You should have left him alone!"

"It's not my fault she couldn't keep Tom home." Julia thought she knew the voice, distinctly female, but it was different somehow; the sound of it refused to fully spark her memory.

Julia risked moving closer, trying to make out who Sandy was arguing with.

"Just stay away from Emily and me or else," Sandy threatened, her voice full of indignation.

The other figure snorted. "You haven't changed. Sandy Edwards, still taking care of her. She should be going to jail for killing him."

Julia climbed further up the grassy bank leading to Drury Lane Books. She wished the light were focused on the street and not the rocky beach.

"Emily wouldn't hurt anyone," Sandy protested protectively. "You don't know what you're talking about. She…"

Julia slipped, causing a muffled commotion as the contents of her bag jostled together, and the conversation cut to silence. By the time she had righted herself, Sandy and the other figure were gone.

Julia dropped onto one of the chairs surrounding the fire pit closest to the bookshop and surveyed the damage to her person. The stray rocks along the slope had caused a few minor scrapes to her knees and elbows, but they didn't sting and irritate as much as spooking off the women had. Julia sighed. *I had to go and ruin it.*

## ~ Chapter 12 ~

The next morning, Julia drove up the Gunflint Trail to the lumber company where Tom Peterson had worked. Turning off the road, she followed the signs towards the office. The deceased man reminded her so much of her soon-to-be ex-husband that she wondered if he had found his mystery lover in the same place Graham had: his place of work.

Parking, she slid out of the car and headed to the door; stepping inside, she found herself in a dark-paneled room with three desks. A young woman not much older than Lucy occupied the desk nearest the door, acting as sentry. Julia waited as she finished taking a message, absentmindedly twirling a long lock of blond hair. When she finished, she glanced at Julia. "May I help you?" she asked, flashing a practiced smile.

It wasn't until that moment Julia realized she didn't have a clue as to what she was going to say. *You wouldn't know who Tom Peterson was having an affair with, would you?*

"Ma'am, are you all right?"

"I'm sorry." *Ma'am? Do I look like a ma'am to you?* "I was just lost in thought." Julia shook the unexpected flash of anger away.

The receptionist smiled again. "Is there something I can help you with?"

"Actually, yes. I was asked to stop by and collect Tom Peterson's personal things." Julia offered her best smile.

"And you are?" The smile faded.

"Sheriff Barrett has been rather busy, so he sent me. It shouldn't take long." She scanned the two desks, one with a nameplate of Carol Foster and the other with Tom Peterson's on one corner. Julia decided forceful might be the best course of action. She moved to step past the young receptionist. "If you could get me a small box, I'm sure I'll be out of your way in just a few minutes."

An irritated huff sounded behind her as the woman dropped her headset and walked through a door to another room.

Julia quickly looked through the desk drawers, but outside of regular office supplies, the desk looked nearly unused. Even the desktop was clean. *At least Graham kept my picture on his desk. A lot of good that did.*

"Is there something I can help you with?" a new voice sounded behind her.

Julia stood, wondering if she was busted. "No, the young lady was just getting a box so I could collect Mr. Peterson's personal effects. I take it you worked with him?"

The well-dressed older woman cocked her head appraisingly. "Yes, Tom and I handled sales. He was one of the best. Well, when he put his mind to it."

Julia found the last comment odd. "What do you mean?"

"It's not good to speak ill of the dead, but Tom paid more attention to the female clients and their receptionists than the job itself. He was attractive and knew how to turn a head, especially the young and pretty ones."

"…and blond," Julia almost growled.

"How'd you know?"

"Sorry… aren't they all? I take it he turned heads here, too?" Her glance darted towards the receptionist's desk.

"Cindy?" The woman rolled her eyes, shifted closer, and lowered her voice. "It wasn't public knowledge, but I came in on them once, getting cozy in the storage room." She shook her head. "His poor wife. I guess she'd finally had enough. That's what you get, I suppose."

Julia thought for a moment, allowing herself to believe that Emily could have done it. *She had every reason to, after all.*

Cindy came back into the room, a box in hand. The freshly applied powder did little to conceal the white lines in her makeup that streams of tears had caused. It seemed Tom Peterson had a knack for making women cry even from beyond the grave. "Here you go." Cindy gingerly handed the box over to Julia.

As the older woman grabbed her purse from the desk facing the window, she called out, "Cindy, I'll be out the rest of the day." She didn't wait for a response before exiting the building.

Julia's brow furrowed, watching the hasty exit. She sat down and started to look through the desk again, this time paying more attention. That was when it struck her—there was nothing personal on it or in it. Not even an old receipt. Either Tom didn't keep personal items in the desk, or someone had already removed them. She stole a glance at Cindy, only to find her back turned.

Julia blew a frustrated breath and started to close the drawer. Just as she did, she noticed a strip of photos, like the kind you get in a photo booth, half-hidden against the side of the drawer. She carefully pulled the strip from its secret spot and shoved it in her pocket. She closed the drawer the rest of the way and stood.

"Thank you." She waved cheerfully at Cindy as she walked by the sorrowful woman with the empty box in hand. In the parking lot, she tossed it in the back seat of her SUV, wanting to flee the scene before anyone was the wiser. She headed back towards town but turned left into to the small trailhead parking area.

Safely stopped, she slipped the picture strip from her pocket and found four shots of Tom cuddled with the receptionist, Cindy, her long blond hair in a ponytail. They were both grinning widely, arms affectionately entangled with one another. "Was she your mystery woman at the boat launch, or were you having multiple affairs?"

*He got what he deserved.* Julia gazed at the simple white T-shirt he was wearing in the photos and couldn't help but imagine a ruby bloom of blood spreading out over the abdomen. Had Emily stabbed him in a fit of rage? One of his jealous lovers? Or had Julia herself played the vindictive assassin during a massive mental breakdown? "Who punished you, Tom Peterson?"

# Broken Promises

## ~ Chapter 13 ~

Not ready to face opening the shop, Julia stopped by Java Moose. She ordered an Irish Breakfast tea and looked for an empty table.

"You can share my table," came a familiar voice.

Julia couldn't place it until she turned to find the older woman from the lumber company office. She collected her cup and headed over. "Thank you." She nodded, sliding into a chair diagonally across from her near the rustic, wood-paneled walls.

"Sure." The woman took a bite of a fruit turnover, flakes of it catching in her lipstick. "My name's Carol Foster."

"Nice to formally meet you," Julia said and then focused on her cup, trying to ignore the odd silence settling between them.

"Did you find what you were looking for?" Carol asked pointedly.

Julia sputtered her tea. "I'm sorry?"

Carol shifted to the seat directly across from Julia. "At the office. I knew a lot about Tom, but I don't remember him having a penchant for antiques."

*Small town.* With a napkin, Julia dabbed the bit of liquid from the table. "Why didn't you say anything while I was there? You could have had me thrown out."

"Who would I tell?" She waved a hand in the air as if it were no big deal. "Cindy? Not likely. I know what kind of guy Tom was. We both grew up here. I was a few years ahead of him, but he and my brother were friends."

Julia felt the need to explain herself. "He was killed with something stolen from my shop. I guess that's why I feel connected to the whole thing. I just wanted to see if I could find something to help figure out who killed him."

"What makes you think it wasn't his wife? She had textbook motive."

"I don't know. I just want to be sure." Julia leaned closer, lowering her voice. "I guess she was right in thinking he was having an affair. Do you really think she could have done it?"

"To be honest, I don't know. I've only ever met Emily through festivals or at the café. I was in Chicago at school when she and Tom started dating but heard all about his behavior."

Julia took a sip from her cup, careful not to make a mess again. "He was friends with your brother."

"Yes—Adam. He moved to New York after graduating from law school. He comes home once a year to visit. He liked Emily—a lot. There isn't anything he wouldn't have done for her, but it just didn't happen. I think that's why he stays away. You don't forget your first love."

Julia swallowed hard. "No, you don't." She paused, allowing a nearby couple to pass out of earshot. "He was seen with a woman at the boat launch at the top of the Gunflint. Do you think it could have been Cindy?"

"I don't know. Maybe. She didn't work to hide her attraction to him, but she was looking for a husband, not a fling. I think she believed Tom would leave Emily for her. She was devastated when we got the call."

Julia nodded. "Seems there were a few women with reason to kill him."

"Motive all around." Carol laughed morbidly, raising her coffee cup in a strange salute.

# Broken Promises

## ~ Chapter 14 ~

Julia spent the rest of the afternoon cleaning the remaining fingerprint dust from every surface in the shop. Whenever she thought she had washed it all away, she'd find a new gray smudge. While she scrubbed, her mind worked through what she'd learned about Tom Peterson, and more so, what she was starting to think about Emily.

Henry sat at the top of the staircase meowing at her. She checked the front door and flipped the light switch as she headed up to feed him.

Sitting on her deck with a glass of wine and a notebook, she wrote down everything she knew about the case. "Emily was afraid Tom was having an affair. Based on what the mystery woman said to Sandy, it was true that he was. It's obvious Sandy doesn't like whoever she is." Julia snorted, talking things over with Henry. "I mean, who would like someone shoving them around,

right? And the feeling seemed mutual from her tone."
She sipped on the wine. "Could this woman in the
shadows be the mistress? If the receptionist, Cindy,
thought he was leaving Emily for her, she would have a
motive, but she didn't know about the letter opener. And
this woman seemed older. Like she knew Sandy and
Emily when they were younger. Accusing her of always
taking care of Emily. The voice did seem familiar, after
all—like I've heard it before, but differently." Feeling an
early fall nip in the air, Julia retreated to the bedroom for
an afghan.

She knelt before the ornately carved wooden hope
chest at the foot of the bed. It was the one thing of Aunt
Sadie's Julia hadn't gone through. The items in the chest
were her aunt's most personal possessions and she
hadn't yet found the courage to face those memories. It
was also where she kept the lilac and rose afghan she
would wrap around Julia when she was a young girl.

Julia opened the lid and examined the items resting
just inside: a small satin-covered box held a collection of
brooches, just a few of the treasures discovered on their
many explorations of estate sales. She had a memory for
most of the small bejeweled treasures. She felt tears sting
and blinked a few times.

Removing the drop shelf, Julia found a dress wrapped in paper. She laid it out on the bed. The yellow linen fabric with mother of pearl buttons along the front looked like it was from the forties. Julia smiled as she carefully rewrapped the dress and knelt back in front of the chest. Just below where the dress had been, she found a large leather-bound scrapbook. When she was younger, Julia would spend hours looking at the photos and newspaper clippings hidden within. Julia marveled at the exciting life her aunt lived. *So many stories I never got to hear.* As she opened the cover, a photograph drifted out onto the floor. Reclaiming it, Julia saw it was a picture of her aunt Sadie wearing the yellow linen dress, standing with another young woman, their arms wrapped around each other as they stood in front of the Eiffel Tower. Smiling at seeing how happy her aunt looked, Julia turned it over. "Paris, August 1944, Me and Charlie." She flipped it back over. "Guess that's your nickname." Julia mused.

Further down, Julia spied the familiar lilac and rose stitching. Removing the one blanket on top, she pulled hers out, the familiar scent of her aunt teased her nostrils. She held the blanket to her and breathed in the scent. As she did so, an envelope tumbled to the floor. Examining the sealed ivory casing, Julia found her name written on one side. Her heart fluttered, recognizing the handwriting instantly, as shaking fingers carefully pried open the seal.

*My Sweet Julia,*

*I'm dead. Obviously so, since you are reading this letter. I knew one day you would want your favourite afghan, so it is my hope that not too much time will pass before you find this. There are things I wanted to… no… should have told you years ago, but time crept by too quickly so now it's left to this. Forgive me for not telling you these things in person. I really did try.*

*First, don't blame yourself for your marriage. We all make choices we sometimes regret; Lord knows, I've made a few of my own. One I will take into eternity, but that isn't your fault. Neither is your marriage. Graham was never good enough for you. I wanted to say something before the wedding but was told to mind my own business. Your mother never liked my meddling with your life, but she can't say anything now.*

Julia chuckled, understanding what her aunt meant about her mother and Graham. She never doubted her mother's love, but Julia was too much a free spirit to fall in line with her every wish. Thinking back, her mother's less-than-excited response about her acceptance to art school sounded a lot like Graham's. "Doesn't matter now." Julia focused on the letter.

*The second thing I need to tell you is going to be difficult to explain, even more so for you to hear, but you need to know. So many times, I used to imagine that you were my daughter. There were even times when I swore you were. You were so much like me and I must confess I enjoyed that, much to your mother's chagrin. Beyond our shared love of antiques and art, there is one other trait… a gift that we share. Something your mother forbade me to speak of. She has always feared anything she doesn't understand. Something she shares with our mother. My dearest Julia, do you remember the trip we took to Nantucket to celebrate your thirteenth birthday? We explored the antique shops and the one estate with the English hedge garden. Do you remember what happened there?*

Furrowing her brow, Julia recalled the event. In fact, she couldn't believe she'd forgotten. They had been shopping for several hours before running across the estate sale. Aunt Sadie was never one to pass up the opportunity to find treasure. Julia had searched through the rooms on the first floor before slipping beyond the velvet rope barrier to the second floor. It wasn't done to intentionally break the rules, she wasn't one to do that. Push the boundaries, yes, but she learned early on how to rebel within given parameters. Something on that day was different. When her aunt asked her later why she left the main floor, Julia couldn't answer. She only knew she felt a pull, a need to go up the dark-carpeted stairs and into the bedroom at the end of the portrait-lined hall. She stood at the doorway, peering into the room, when a glint of something caught her eye. The pull grew stronger and beckoned her to enter. Julia crossed the room, her Mary Janes gliding over the plush crimson carpet. The glimmer came from a small silver box with a rose press-formed in the top. As she traced her finger over the delicate lines of the rose, the box opened. To her delight, she had triggered the hidden latch. The top opened to reveal a small silver band with a freshwater pearl nestled in tiny silver rose petals. Julia knew it was wrong to touch the ring, it was wrong to be in the bedroom, but she picked it up and slipped it on her finger. It was so inviting, and it was only for a moment, after all. As soon as the band reached her knuckle, the room started to spin and heat flooded her, sending Julia to the floor. When Julia collapsed, the last thing she remembered seeing was a little girl in a blue dress with a ribbon at the waist and puffed sleeves standing near her, smiling and asking if she wanted to play.

Julia pulled the afghan around her shoulders as the memory wove its way through her. She hadn't thought of that time in years, but now the memories flooded in, and she remembered waking on that red carpet to find her aunt speaking softly to her.

"Don't sit up too quickly. It's all right now," her aunt soothed.

Julia's eyes darted around the room. "Wh... what happened? Where'd she go?"

"Where did who go?" Sadie asked.

"The little girl." Julia started to cry, emotion overtaking her although she couldn't understand why. "I'm sorry. I only wanted to see the box, and inside there was a little ring." She sat up, tears of guilt and fear falling.

Sadie wrapped her arms around Julia, cuddling her close. "It's all right. Tell me exactly what happened."

Julia remembered telling her aunt everything. She looked down; the ring was gone. "Aunt Sadie, I swear it happened just like I said. The ring was silver with a pearl sitting in the petals of a rose. The little girl... she looked like she walked out of one of your history books. Then everything went dark and I woke up with you. Do you know what happened?"

Julia remembered considering her aunt's blue eyes, seeing them cloud over with worry and an internal struggle. Even at her young age, Julia was able to discern another person's feelings, though she wasn't always able to understand them. Sadie had taken Julia's hands in hers and said, "I know it seems frightening, but it's a gift, really."

"A gift?" young Julia had asked.

"You and I, we can see and feel things that others can't." Aunt Sadie's jaw opened and shut as she tried to choose words that would fit what had happened. "We don't have to talk about it now; your mother will be expecting us back. But I'll explain everything to you when you need to know, and if you want to ask me anything, my door is always open."

Julia was still frightened. She had simply wanted to put the chilling event behind her, and that's just what she had done. She didn't speak of it with her aunt again or even think of it until now when the old memory resurfaced—painstakingly drawn up to the forefront of her mind like a long-sunken anchor.

Julia shook the cobwebs off the memory and the others that started to prick at her. Those moments when

Sadie attempted to bring up the subject again, only to be met by closed ears. At those moments she was more like her mother than her aunt. Julia brushed a tear away and turned her attention back to the letter.

*I'm not sure how to say it, but to put it on the table, the ring you found had a curse, of sorts. Now before you shake your head and tell me I'm crazy, hear me out. The little girl you saw was a shadow. I saw her too but didn't know how to begin to explain it to you then. Sometimes objects that are precious to us in life hold a piece of us in death. Most of the time, this is by accident and without malicious intent. The owner of the ring died at a young age after a long illness and was still mischievous. You felt it when you put the ring on your finger. That, my sweet girl, is the gift we share. We can sense the energy within an object – its spirit, if you will. It is a gateway to the past.*

*Now, you need to listen carefully. Sometimes the energy within an object isn't benign. Objects can be cursed and until the curse is broken, it will endure. The ring needed the memory of the child released to be safe again, but others won't be so simple.*

*There are two books in my library to help you get started. They have been my constant companions and I*

*have filled their pages with bits of lore and knowledge*
*I've collected over my long years. You'll recognize them.*
*Look to them for answers and no matter what, be careful.*

*All my love,*
*Sadie*

Dropping back against the pine memory chest, Julia was at a loss. "Oh, Sadie, I'm sorry I didn't listen to you then." Julia reread the letter several times, letting each word sink in. *Could Aunt Sadie's letter be the key to what's going on around here?* Hearing a noise, she headed to the deck, the afghan still pulled around her protectively. Julia watched Henry make his way along the lower roof up to her. "Finally get hungry?" She sat on the Adirondack chair, and the large orange tabby jumped gracefully onto her lap. Julia cuddled with him, scratching the ear with the missing piece. "So, my little alley warrior, what's the answer?"

Henry mewed.

Julia kissed him on the head. "Not very helpful. I wish you could talk. Maybe then I'd know what to do about all of this. It's one thing to have the shop broken into and a murder, but now I'm some ghost whisperer or something?" She picked up the large cat carrying him into the kitchen as she continued the one-sided conversation. "It's ridiculous. I'm nothing special, and Sadie was a bit odd. Maybe she's wrong or it's the last bit of a joke."

Henry looked at her, dismissing her last statement with a knowing expression.

"All right, Your Majesty. If you know so much, why don't you explain it to me," Julia challenged.

Henry meowed again, this time sounding a bit frustrated.

"Forgive me for not understanding cat-speak. Go have your dinner then." Julia put him on the floor before going back out to the deck. Taking her spot again, she grabbed the notebook off the side table. "One problem at a time. I need to figure out who broke into the shop and killed Tom Peterson. Aunt Sadie's letter will have to wait." She flipped through the notes she had already made and jotted down the questions plaguing her mind. Julia sketched out a flow chart to see who and what connected. "Nothing was disturbed, other than the lamp. Whoever came in knew what they were looking for, but who knew the letter opener existed and where to find it?" Only three names connected to the letter opener. Julia checked everything again, and it all came back to those three names.

"Lucy, Emily, or me." Nothing made sense about it, though. Lucy wouldn't hurt a fly, and Emily just didn't seem the type. "Besides, she thinks *I* did it." Julia stared out at the dark sky, watching lightning flash in the distance. *Did I?* As the white-hot bolts sizzled over the water, she realized she couldn't solve this problem without all the answers. Perhaps it was time to talk to Lucy. Maybe she could get a better idea of who was in the shop that day, who had access to the letter opener.

# Broken Promises

# ~ Chapter 15 ~

Julia paced the shop, dusting and adjusting displays, waiting for Lucy to arrive. She'd spent the night barely sleeping, her mind in a constant war over the idea that there was something she was missing. It was hard to imagine anyone breaking into the shop to steal the letter opener just to use it to kill Tom Peterson. Julia's mind was a spinning top. "Why would anyone want to frame me?"

*Unless you did it.* Nagging doubts crept in. Remembering what happened years before wasn't helping. Julia had no memory of anything after she put the tiny silver ring on her finger and then woke in her aunt's arms.

"Alright, let's be logical about this. That was a long time ago and has nothing to do with the here and now." She wanted desperately to eliminate herself from the suspect list.

Hearing the grandfather clock chime 12:30, Julia headed to the front of the shop. Lucy was half an hour late, something that was wildly out of character for her. Standing at the window, Julia looked down the empty street worrying that something might have happened, some illness or injury that had caused her to delay. She was just about to give her a call when the bell above the door rang, snatching Julia out of her grim thoughts.

Lucy closed the door, her usual bright smile missing as she approached Julia. She dropped her bag and threw her arms around Julia's neck. "I was so worried about you. I thought you'd been arrested. I'm sorry I'm late. I called, but it kept going straight to voicemail."

"I turned my phone off and forgot to turn it back on," Julia explained. "I'm sorry to worry you."

Lucy offered a pale smile. "I'm glad everything's all right."

"Why are you late? That's not like you."

Lucy's smile faded. "I was up late—couldn't sleep. My mom and I argued again and, well, I need to talk to you."

Julia slipped her arm around Lucy's shoulder. "Come on. Let's sit down and talk." She led Lucy to the back of the shop. "Would you like something to drink?"

Lucy stared at the floor but nodded.

"I'll be right back." Julia headed to the teapot she kept in the shop and poured two cups. The bell above the door rang. Taking the cups to the desk, she told Lucy, "I'll see to the customer, you drink the tea."

Reaching the front of the shop, Julia put on her best smile—one that was meant to hide the stress of a divorce in progress, being a suspect in a homicide investigation, and her aunt's strange note about curses. "Welcome to Past Imperfect. Is there anything special you're looking for today?"

Two older women stood before her, all grins and wide-eyed gaping. "No... no... just looking. Are you the owner?"

"Yes, I am." Julia watched as the women exchanged knowing glances; her stomach twisted. The bell above the door rang out again as another group entered the shop. Julia greeted the two new couples warmly as well. Any other day she would have welcomed the traffic, but now it seemed the gawkers from the café had relocated to her shop. Julia was relieved when Lucy appeared from the back to help. Their tea and chat would have to wait.

The steady stream of nosey visitors kept Julia and Lucy busy for a while without many sales. Julia dropped wearily into her desk chair, her untouched tea now cold.

She didn't appreciate the whispers and stares but didn't know what to do about it, either.

"I put up the *Closed* sign."

"Thanks, Lucy. I'm sorry we didn't get a chance to talk. Do you have time now or did you need to go?"

"Mom's out, so I can stay a little longer. Besides, I need to apologize to you."

"Apologize? For what?"

"For lying to you."

Julia looked at Lucy, unsure whether she had misread her completely. "What about?"

Lucy sat in the other chair. "The other day you asked me about the letter opener."

"I remember." Julia forced herself to stay calm.

"After you left for lunch, I went into your desk and took the letter opener out of the box. I wanted to look at it again. It was just so beautiful. Then my mom came in, and some customers, too," Lucy blurted. "I didn't have time to put it back in the desk drawer until after everyone left."

Julia sighed. "It's okay. I was going to ask you about that. Were the customers anyone you recognized?" *It seems the list of people who knew where to find it is growing.*

"No, I can't even remember their faces. I was upset with my mom and I wasn't focused." Lucy was on the verge of tears. "The sheriff asked me all kinds of questions about that day, the customers, the letter opener, *you*. I thought maybe it had been stolen and I was being accused of taking it or something."

"I'm sorry you got caught up in all of this." Julia opened the desk drawer and showed Lucy the empty box. "Someone stole the letter opener and used it to kill Tom Peterson. I can hardly believe it myself."

Lucy's eyes grew wide. "That's just awful! Who would do such a thing?"

Julia put the box back in the drawer. "That's what I've been trying to figure out. I don't like the idea that someone used something of mine for such a terrible deed. I was hoping you could help out, maybe remember something that would clear everything up."

"I wish I could," Lucy said as she looked down sadly, "but the police have gone over everything with me and I just don't remember much. I'm not even sure the customers who came in were local."

Julia had an idea. It was so simple, she couldn't believe it hadn't occurred to her before. "We should check the purchase logs. We might find someone's name there."

Lucy put a hand on Julia's arm. "The police already did that. There were two purchases, both for cash. Old ladies if I remember correctly, but it's all a blur."

Julia sighed, deflated. "I think someone is trying to frame me for killing Tom Peterson."

Lucy's eyes were like saucers. "That's crazy. Why would you kill him? You mean just because it's your letter opener?"

"I don't know. I've never met the man, but whoever killed him wants me involved." Taking a chance, Julia questioned, "Did you happen to know him?"

Lucy gave her a strange look. "Not very well. But I knew enough to know that he was kissing someone who wasn't his wife."

Julia looked at Lucy with hope. "When did you see this?"

"Walking past the Peterson house last week. It was dark, so I couldn't see her face, but they were kissing at the front door. When the door opened, I saw blond hair. I know Mrs. Peterson has dark hair."

"They went inside?"

Lucy nodded. "I don't know why, but I watched from the edge of the driveway, hidden by the tall bushes. It was wrong, I know, but yeah, they went inside."

"And you don't have any idea who she was? Could it have been a friend and maybe Emily was already home?" Julia wanted to be positive of what the young woman had witnessed.

"Not with the way they were kissing." Lucy's expression darkened, clearly bothered by it all.

Julia fell into thought. Could Lucy have seen Tom with Cindy that night? When she realized a long silence had fallen between them, she broke it by saying, "Why don't you head home? It's been a long day, and you deserve a break. I've got some things to take care of, anyway."

"Sure." Lucy nodded, looking relieved. "Did you want me to come in earlier tomorrow to help set up for the festival crowd?"

"That'd be great, I'm glad you thought of it." Julia walked Lucy to the door and locked it behind her. Heading upstairs, she watched the sun paint the sky in shades of pink and orange. "It's bad enough to have an affair, but to take them to the house you share with your wife?" It brought up old fears and dark imaginings from Julia's marriage. She couldn't help but wonder whether Graham had taken advantage of her absence to have a woman at the house. *You left him.* The little voice pricked at her conscience again. "That doesn't change anything," she spat back.

Julia was determined to ignore her inner voice and work on something more productive. She was trying to pluck up the courage to do the only thing she could think of – investigate the Peterson house.

# Broken Promises

## ~ Chapter 16 ~

Julia parked her blue SUV along the darkened corner one block north of the Peterson house. With her hair tucked up in a loose bun and wearing a dark wool sweater, and slacks, she was sure she would go unnoticed. There were only a few low-lit lampposts along the residential streets and little moonlight to cast shadows. Julia grabbed a pair of black leather gloves off the passenger seat. They weren't the sleek type a character about to break into a crime scene would wear in a movie, but Julia hadn't brought all her possessions north and could only find an old pair of leather work gloves. Slipping the pair on, she found them to be at least a size too large and better designed for a man's hands. "At least I won't leave fingerprints." Taking a deep breath, she climbed out of her car and made her way along the street, avoiding the dull pools of lamplight and sticking to the cover of inky darkness.

The Peterson house was dark and still, with no movement or illumination behind the street-facing windows. Julia avoided the front door and walked carefully around to the back. In the dim light offered by accent torches lining the yard and deck, Julia could make out a patio area with chairs and a metal fire pit. There were potted plants, still blooming, scattered around the patio and yard. She imaged what life would have been for Tom and Emily when they first moved here. The beautiful backyard must have offered such promise and hope; it seemed a lovely place to spend a cool fall evening with friends while talking and laughing around the fire.

Julia didn't find a back door. Instead, she was met with a sliding glass panel and metal screen. The latter slid open, but the heavy glass door refused to budge. "So much for making this easy." To her right was a wood-framed sash window. Checking it, Julia found it moved up easily. "Odd not to have a screen." Leaning forward, she tumbled into the kitchen near the dining room. She brushed herself off as she got to her feet. Taking a step, she froze. *Window.* Julia turned back and slid it closed. Pulling the small flashlight from her pocket, she moved the beam over the floor, trying to keep the light out of the windows.

Her eyes followed the yellow sliver as it cut a slash through the dark, dancing over the dining room table's floral centerpiece that begged for its thirst to be quenched. Julia looked past it, knowing the house had been empty since everything happened. She got a bit of a chill imagining the horrible act that had taken place here, and a rush of adrenaline had her worried over her part in all of it. *Which room had he bled out in?*

A pine sideboard, filled with dishes, lined one wall. "Wedding gifts," she mused, refusing to see her own life in the cabinet. Sketches hung on either side of the rectangular furniture piece, one of main street and the other of Lake Superior. She examined the well-done sketches and found the initials *S.E.* in the lower right corner. "Well, S.E., you're very talented." She looked closer at the initials. "Sandy?" A soft gasp of surprise passed her lips as a smile formed.

Julia moved into the living room, pleasantly arranged with oversized furniture covered with a rose-colored pattern and a wingback chair with an afghan draped over it. The room was cozy; even in the low light, Julia could see the personal touches that define a home. A cluster of photographs on an upright piano drew her attention. She looked over each of the memories of happier times. Tom Peterson's expression reminded her of Graham—that cocky, self-assured smirk—especially during the last year of their marriage. The depths into which their relationship had drained, simply going through the motions, though Julia knew Graham would argue that point. He liked to pretend everything was rosy. She wondered if the same had happened to Emily and Tom. She felt guilty examining their lives uninvited, but jail was a strong possibility in her future—one Julia didn't want to see come true. If she couldn't solve this, then that's exactly where she could end up.

Headlights appeared outside, flickering through the curtains, and Julia dropped to the floor, trying to silence the drum thudding in her chest and hoping they'd continue past. Once gone, she turned on the flashlight again, gasping when she noticed where she was kneeling. The off-white carpet melted into a brown stain below her. Julia jumped back into a side table, knocking over a lamp. *Pull yourself together.* She checked the lamp, relieved it wasn't broken, and returned it to its proper place. "What am I doing? Acting like I'm one of Charlie's Angels or something."

She headed down the hallway, opening the first door—a closet. The next door presented a set of stairs.

Julia shined the light down to find a beige carpet. She crept downward to discover a basement room, a bit larger than the living room. Panning the light around the room, she noticed immediately how different this room was from the rest of the house. The furniture was dark leather and very masculine in design. On the far wall hung a dartboard, like those found in a bar, and to the left was a dark wood counter long enough to support three stools. Stepping closer, she could see two pull taps with different brands of local craft beers, as well as a mini fridge. On the opposite wall, a large flat-screen television was mounted into the dark paneling. The sofa and matching leather recliner faced the television. It had all the trappings of a typical man cave.

Julia walked around the room, taking it all in, wondering if she were really that different from Emily. Graham always wanted to turn their basement into a room much like the one Julia stood in. Every so often, he would threaten to throw out the junk stored over the years, but when it came to it, the room continued to do its job and house their memories.

Julia was so lost in thought that she almost missed it when the flashlight beam drifted over the carpet and caught a glint of metal flickering in its wake. She stooped down and searched for the object, reaching out when the light finally found it again. The work gloves made grasping the small item difficult. She pulled one off in frustration and claimed the flat, round piece of metal. Turning it over in her palm, Julia examined it. One edge curved smoothly, but the other was jagged, with a shape cut from the center. It resembled the type of coin that couples give to one another. This silver coin looked to be the male half, with a stag head next to the cutout of a doe's head. The small ring that a chain would slip through was missing. "I wonder who has the other piece." She didn't have time to guess since footsteps sounded on the floor above. Julia jerked her head up, on high alert. *Damn.* She pocketed the coin and looked for another way out.

She followed along the wall, panic rising as no alternate exit became apparent. She moved behind the bar, hoping for a place to hide. A crack in the wall offered a sliding panel that housed a small storage closet. She slipped inside and closed the panel. Julia pressed against the wall; she could see light filter through the narrow opening where the panel didn't close completely. Julia shrank back as someone entered the room. Her breath caught, noticing her bare hand and realizing that she'd left the glove behind. She barely had a memory of placing it on the floor as she examined her find. Taking a chance, Julia leaned closer to the opening, hoping to see who was in the room. Her view, partially obstructed by the bar, afforded her no answers. The only clue was muffled, angry cursing from someone that sounded like a woman. Julia stood to see more of the room, but she couldn't see who had come in.

"Damn it, where is it?" she barked in anger.

From the direction of her voice, Julia assumed the woman was crouched on the floor, right where her glove was. *The coin. She must be searching for it.*

"I can't believe I loved you. Worse..." the words trailed off in wracked sobs.

*What worse?* Julia's curiosity outweighed her fear of being caught. She continued to watch; after a few moments, the woman stood but kept her back to the bar. Julia frowned, noticing the stranger's hair and face were obscured by a baseball cap. She couldn't even gauge hair or skin color from her awkward vantage point. She was certain there was something familiar about her.

The woman looked around the room slowly, with the pace of memories unfolding. Several more minutes passed before she headed for the stairs, flipping a switch and sending Julia back into darkness.

Julia braced herself against the wall and released the breath she'd been holding. She could hear footfalls on the floor above and waited until it was quiet again. Julia turned the words over in her mind, and something familiar pricked at her memory. Time dragged; finally, the house was quiet again. Sliding the door open, Julia clicked the flashlight on and ran to where she'd left her glove, hoping it was still there. Searching desperately, she scanned the floor, finding nothing but carpet. "No. Come on." Panic snaked its way through her. After several moments, she found it sticking out from beneath the sofa. The mysterious woman who had visited the basement must have kicked it by mistake. Grabbing it, she sheathed her hand again and made her way back to the main level.

Julia exited through the same window, landing this time on the pine deck. She turned and closed it, making certain everything was as she'd found it. She crept back around the house, pocketing her flashlight and the coin. Once back in her car, she let out her breath and tore off the gloves, shoving them in the dash compartment. Turning the engine over, she made her way past the Peterson house before heading left onto the next block. Julia gave the house one last look, a dismal sadness spreading over her before she entered town from the main highway, hoping no one had noticed her.

## ~ Chapter 17 ~

Making her way down Wisconsin Avenue, Julia saw Emily and Sandy outside the Gunflint Tavern. She stopped at the intersection harder than intended, feeling the straps of her seat belt press into her body as she lurched forward. *Sandy's quarrel with the woman in the shadows!* "That's where I've heard the voice before." She scanned the area for a parking spot, but the incoming flow of people driving in for the music festival had filled up the normally quiet street, forcing Julia to park at Past Imperfect and walk back to the tavern. "Whoever I saw her arguing with was just in the Peterson house, I know it!" Julia felt a rush of something akin to excitement as she spoke to herself. *Am I close to finding out the answers I need?*

Julia looked for Emily outside the tavern but didn't see either her or Sandy. She headed up the stone steps and through the glass door, her senses overwhelmed by a boisterous hubbub and the smell of grilling food. The Gunflint Tavern wasn't overly large, having only a dozen or so tables clustered before a long wood bar. A large chalkboard, covering the right wall, served as the menu, and colorful local art was displayed all around. The establishment may have been in a small Midwestern town, but the food never reflected it. The menu offered an unexpected variety of culinary delights to tempt any visitor. During the weekends, the tavern could be packed with out-of-towners enjoying locally brewed craft beer, but weeknights were left to the locals. Tonight, the crowd was a bit larger than expected, most likely due to the upcoming music festival. Julia spotted Sandy standing alone at the end of the bar. There was an empty stool next to her so, taking a deep breath, Julia strolled towards her.

She had almost reached her intended destination when the bartender, Diane, plunked two bottles from the local brewery in front of Sandy and stood by to chat. Julia shifted a step, moving against the bar to wait a few seats down from the women. She gave a friendly nod to an older man next to her while nervous wings fluttered and beat the insides of her stomach wall. It was hard not to be worked up after almost being caught at the Peterson house, and now she was working on another bold idea: trying to get information from Sandy and Emily.

Julia watched Sandy chat with the bartender; their posture was relaxed and friendly. At one point, Diane dropped a comforting hand on Sandy's forearm, her smile warm and bright. Nothing in their behavior suggested that earlier they could have been arguing to the extent of a physical altercation. In fact, their manner towards one another could be viewed as amiable—intimate, even.

Julia couldn't make out their exact words over the din, and suddenly she was suffering a tinge of guilt for spying on them. It didn't help that she felt she was sticking out in the crowd, so turning, she ordered a glass of wine from one of the servers in hopes of blending in.

"Julia." Halfway through Julia's seasonal North Shore wine, Sandy's voice cut through the noise of the room.

"Hi!" Julia was a bit startled, catching a dribble of wine on her chin before she waved.

Sandy motioned Julia over as she took a long sip from her bottle of beer.

Julia collected her glass of wine and made her way over. An odd expression seemed to pass over Sandy's face, but Julia couldn't tell what it meant. *Wistful* was the best word to describe it. "Out enjoying the evening?" Julia asked.

"Something like that. What about you? I don't think I've ever seen you in anything but flowy skirts and blouses," Sandy commented, looking Julia up and down. "You've always reminded me of a genteel lady straight out of a romance novel."

"I went for a walk along the beach." Julia blushed. "I guess autumn is coming a little early."

"It should be a beauty."

Julia agreed, sipping her wine as she tried to think of what to say next. "Are you drinking for two?" she asked nonchalantly, gesturing at the extra beer.

"What? Oh, that's for Em. She went next door for a minute," Sandy explained.

Taking the opportunity, Julia prodded, "Why do you think so many people seem to agree that Emily is better off without Tom?"

Sandy pulled the bottle abruptly from her lips. "Because he wasn't good enough for her."

"What do you mean?" Julia pressed.

"They met in high school. He was the star running back and the guy that just about every girl wanted to date." Sandy rolled her eyes and took a swig. "Emily was so different than he was, quiet and shy. They started dating in our junior year. He was a cheating bastard then, but she refused to see it. Em never believed anything negative about Tom. Not even from me," she said bitterly. She took a long drink from the bottle and motioned to Diane for another.

"So you knew something that she didn't?"

"They'd been dating for about a month," Sandy went on. "He had her twisted around his finger. I found him under the bleachers getting cozy with one of the cheerleaders. I told Emily about it, and she confronted him. Tom lied and told her I was mistaken about the whole thing and that I was just jealous. Hard to mistake her head in his lap. Either way, she believed him and not me." She grabbed the new bottle as soon as Diane delivered it. Taking a long drink to wash away the bitter memory, she looked at Julia again. "I had to make a choice: I could keep telling her about him and lose my best friend or keep my mouth shut. I chose the latter."

"That couldn't have been easy for you." Julia's own bitter memories stabbed at her as she mused over the parallels between her life and Emily's.

Sandy snorted and gave a heavy shrug.

"So, you think he was having an affair currently?" Julia asked. "I mean, before he was killed?"

Sandy didn't miss a beat. "Yes, I do."

"You don't have any idea who she could have been?"

"No, of course I don't!" Sandy spat angrily.

Julia focused on her glass of wine, turning it at the stem.

"I'm sorry, you didn't deserve that. I'm just angry that it had to—" Sandy cut herself off mid-sentence.

Emily appeared through the doorway to Sandy's left. She slid onto the bar stool on her opposite side. "Thanks for this." She held up the sweaty brew, tipping it against Sandy's bottle. When she spotted Julia, her eyes widened in surprise.

Julia felt the air thicken, acutely aware that she was unwanted, so she drained her glass of wine and pulled a few dollars from her pocket.

Sandy rested her hand on Julia's forearm lightly. "I'll take care of it."

A protest welled up inside her, but Julia only smiled in acceptance of her friendly gesture. "Thank you." She slipped off the bar stool. "I'd better get going. I have some work to do before opening the shop tomorrow. Have a good night, both of you." Julia didn't wait for a response. She headed to the stairs connecting the Gunflint Tavern to the small timber-framed bar, The Raven, that led to the lower exit.

The last few days turned over in her mind as she walked the short distance back home. Clues were all around, yet she was unable to piece them together. Julia pulled the deer-head coin from her pocket, running the fingertips of one hand over the surface while she steered with the opposite one. "If you were only an affair, why would you give something like this?"

Cutting through the bank parking lot, Julia passed Beth's Fudge and Gifts to get to her own shop. A familiar black Challenger was parked carelessly next to her own car. She stopped at the corner of Beth's, her heart pounding in her chest. She glanced back, trying to decide if she could move without being seen. It was too late; she watched as a figure exited the car, staring at her.

*Graham.*

# Broken Promises

## ~ Chapter 18 ~

Julia took her keys from her pocket and asked in a vexed tone, "What are you doing here?" Mentally she resolved not to allow herself to capitulate to anything he wanted as she'd been accustomed to doing in the past.

"Is that any way to greet your husband?" Graham snapped the car door closed, extending his arms wide as Julia came around to the driver's side.

"I didn't expect you." Julia shifted as he closed the distance to kiss her. "It's a long drive from the Cities."

"You hung up on me, so I came to check on you. I was worried about you, Juls." Graham pulled her into a hug. He ignored her tensing up, stroking her rigid back with his palms.

Graham's touch felt grating and made her skin crawl with irritation. Julia pulled away, breaking the contact.

"I've been busy. I'm fine. You didn't need to drive all the way up here."

"Look, we need to talk. It's time you came home. I miss you." Graham oozed charm when he wanted his way, and this moment was no different. He reached out to pull her against him a second time, using his strong arms to envelop her.

"*Miss* me?" Julia bear-hugged the anger she'd held for years, snapping at him as she pushed back against his chest to extricate herself from his grip once more. "You're only worried about your reputation, afraid of what other people might think. You don't miss *me*; you miss someone to clean, cook, and do your laundry. You miss having a waitress for your football weekends or a date to take to your office parties."

"Here we go again." Graham tossed his arms in the air, the charismatic smile melting into a strained frown.

"You know what, I'd really rather not get into this right now." Julia's fingers rubbed at her throbbing temples. "Graham, I'm tired. I just want to go to bed and forget the day."

"My Julia." Graham stepped in close, his voice like velvet. "It's no wonder. You've been up here all alone, trying to run this shop. I know, I sometimes forget how hard things have been on you. I just want to take care of you, baby." He wasn't forceful this time when he touched her, reaching out tentatively to massage her upper arms and shoulders.

Julia felt her resolve slipping.

Graham's happy expression had returned; he was regarding her with a sultry twinkle in his eyes as he eased her against his chest.

*Damn it.* There was no denying that Julia was in need of physical comfort. Her muscles were in knots from the stress over the murder and her dissolving marriage. It would be so easy to fall into Graham's secure, capable arms and let him take control of her life again. It would be so simple to hand over the reins of her existence and let him call the shots. But even if he could fix the mess she was in, Julia wasn't ready to shut off her mind and heart and go back to living life as her husband's obedient little cookie-cutter wife.

"Let's go inside." Graham slid his arm around Julia's shoulders and guided her towards the shop. Graham hadn't gone more than a step when his pocket exploded with the song "Amie" by Pure Prairie League.

Julia wrenched herself away from the circle of his arms. She would never forget the last time she heard that tune play from his phone. Graham had forgotten the device at home that day and when Julia heard the soft country-rock song belt out into the kitchen, she answered—only to hear a young female voice on the other end. "May I speak to Graham?" the feminine voice had asked.

"This is his wife, Julia," she identified herself. "He isn't here right now, but is there a message I could take for him?"

There was a slight hesitation—the sound of breath—before the line went dead. Julia could only stare at the phone as every alarm bell in her instincts sounded. That evening, she'd realized her suspicions were right when she confronted her husband about the odd phone call. He had denied it, of course, but not before stuttering and stammering his way into the ground. It had taken a few more weeks and a smattering of heart-wrenching clues before he'd admitted his indiscretion outright, apologizing profusely and swearing it was over.

Julia didn't know whether Graham was still having an affair, but hearing that ringtone was like ripping stitches from a wound. If he was still maintaining a relationship with this woman, it would be all the more difficult to forgive. She felt a bit sick that she had ever let him touch her, and any inclination to fall back into his arms was snuffed out in a breath of wind.

"Juls, it's nothing," Graham assured her. He clicked *Decline* on the call and tossed the phone through his open car window. There was a thud as it bounced against the leather bucket seat.

"Nothing?" Julia was infuriated. "How can it be nothing if she's still calling you?"

Displeasure tugged at the corner of Graham's smile. "We're friends, that's all. Don't be dramatic. There's nothing going on between us anymore."

"You get calls from the woman you had a fling with and then accuse *me* of being dramatic?" Julia knew she was yelling, but she no longer cared.

Graham reached over and captured her shoulders, giving her a little shake. "Stop it. Go up and pack a bag; we'll drive back tonight."

Julia tried to pull away from his tense fingers. "No, I'm not going back."

A car moving slowly towards the lake bathed them in blinding light. Graham was quick to let Julia go as the light washed over them, the car stopping and trapping them in the headlights. "Who's this?" he asked in his favorite snarky tone.

"Mrs. Crawford?" Jack Barrett climbed out of the car and stepped easily towards them. "Are you all right?"

Julia didn't know whether to be relieved or cry. "Yes, I'm all right. I was just heading inside." She watched his eyes fall on Graham, measuring him up.

"And you are?" the sheriff asked.

"Her husband." Graham folded his arms across his chest, trying to look bulkier.

Julia rolled her eyes at the display, and the throbbing in her temples doubled. It didn't help seeing Jack Barrett's expression falter with Graham's leg-lifting. "He was just leaving."

Graham whipped his head towards her. "I think I should stay. You haven't been yourself lately."

The sudden mantle of loving husband fell flat, like an actor botching his lines and breaking character. "I'm fine. I'm going upstairs and heading to bed." Julia glanced at Sheriff Barrett, hoping he would intervene — though on what grounds, she didn't know.

"It appears the lady prefers to be alone." There was a warning note in the sheriff's tone.

"I don't remember asking your opinion," Graham snapped, "unless coming between a husband and wife is common in this town."

"Folks usually stay where they are wanted," the sheriff responded with an assured ease.

As Julia watched the two men verbally spar, she slipped her hand into her pocket and felt the half coin. Her mind was recalling painful events, forcing her to relive the late-night calls, odd-scented perfume, and now the jarring ringtone of her husband's lover. That call tonight was enough, the final straw. "Stop it! I'm going inside. Graham, go back to the Cities." Julia headed to the shop, disappearing inside. She fell back against the door, hearing Graham still arguing with the sheriff. She swiped away tears, engaged the lock, and made her way up the stairs to the apartment. The engine of Graham's Challenger revved before he left, tires squealing angrily. Julia couldn't help but wonder whether he'd even want anything to do with her if he knew about the visions inside her head—the dark voice and all that blood. *Maybe he'll leave me alone for good if I tell him about it.* While the idea tempted her, she didn't trust Graham not to have her committed involuntarily if she did. *He'd happily milk the sympathy it would bring.*

Julia forced her thoughts away from the macabre subject and fell onto the bed, exhausted. It didn't last long, however, because a faint but insistent meow beckoned her to the back door. "Good evening, Your Highness." Henry brushed against her leg as he entered, ready for dinner. Julia prepared Henry's dish, petting him while he enjoyed his meal.

"So much has happened," Julia murmured to the cat, "and I'm no closer to understanding what's going on than I was yesterday." She pulled the half coin from her pocket and placed it on the counter. "It's obvious this was more than a fling, at least to one member of the party." She sighed. "Either way, why break into the shop just to steal the letter opener to kill someone? There are other weapons out there. Most Grand Marais residents own some sort of gun."

*Why search when you already know the answers?*

Julia jerked, startled at the whisper in her mind. She glanced around the room just to be sure she was alone and wasn't surprised when she confirmed that only she and her cat were in the room. "The letter opener… what *is* it about that letter opener?" she thought aloud. "It arrived with that odd little note and no clue as to where it really came from, yet I get the feeling it's the most important puzzle piece in this case."

Henry mewed in response.

Julia shook her head. "You know the answer, don't you? You're just keeping it to yourself."

He mewed again, pushing his head against her hand.

Julia scratched his scarred ear. "Maybe I missed something in Aunt Sadie's letter." She kissed the tomcat on his head and returned to the bedroom. Julia kicked off her shoes and, lying back on the bed, she reread the letter. Her eyes repeatedly read the passage about their day out years earlier.

Julia sat upright. "Her library."

Crawling off the bed, Julia headed down to the shop. Bookshelves lined the wall behind the desk Julia used as an office. The shelves were filled with various books, from classic fiction to first edition non-fiction works. Julia recognized many of these books from her shopping adventures with Sadie, but they were for sale and not part of Sadie's personal library. Opening a narrow door, Julia flipped on the light switch, revealing a small storage closet. Wooden crates were stacked along the right wall, each crate marked with its contents. The left wall housed a vertical rack holding large pieces of artwork and a bookshelf. Julia scanned the shelves, finding two oversized leather-bound volumes that caught her eye. She sat on the floor and pulled them into her lap, carefully opening the first worn cover and flipping through the crinkly pages.

Each yellowed page contained stories and images from the past—a collection of condensed tales marked by tragedy and drama.

# Broken Promises

# ~ Chapter 19 ~

Julia rubbed her eyes and glanced at the wall clock near her desk. The clockwork would soon chime one, which explained why her legs were cramping up. She had been so engrossed in her reading that she hadn't moved from her spot on the floor in the storage closet. She had already been through one bound volume and now she was beginning to scan through the next. By now, the task seemed pointless, but she continued to turn the pages. Finally, she stopped at one titled *The Betrayal of Elizabeth Chambers*. The story, like the others, was handwritten, with small sketches in the margins. This particular one had a sketch that caught Julia's eye. Just beneath the title was a pencil drawing of a letter opener, identical to the antique one in question. *That's it!* Julia grabbed notepaper to mark the page and carried the book upstairs.

A few minutes later, she poured herself a cup of tea and curled onto the bed in a tank-style cotton nightgown. "Now, Elizabeth, let's hope your story can give some answers to what's going on."

*The story of Elizabeth Chambers starts on the streets of Paris, 1784. Lizzie was beautiful, with raven hair, green eyes, and the complexion of nobility. Her eyes ensnared men easily; more than one rich man's pockets were bared by her charms. One such man, Thomas, the eldest son of Lord Chambers, wished to claim Lizzie for his own. Thomas was struck with two problems—the first was his father. Lord Chambers was a traditional man and would never accept Lizzie. The second was Lizzie herself. As beautiful as she was, she was of the streets, a common woman, and wild at heart.*

*It took only one night for Thomas to promise her the world. He slipped a ring on her finger and dressed her in fine garments. He taught Lizzie to be the perfect lady in public, but in private, Thomas enjoyed the wild heart. Three months later, he and Elizabeth sailed to England to Lord Chambers' estate. Thomas told Elizabeth as they rode in the gilded carriage, "All of this will be mine... ours, my love. When my father meets you, he will fall in love, and everything will be perfect."*

*Elizabeth saw the life she wanted laid before her, with its tree-lined road and large estate house. Thomas was handsome enough and he did lavish her with gifts and clothing. The others in the house where she worked had been jealous over their whirlwind romance, and Elizabeth couldn't blame them. She, too, would have been envious in their place, toiling as simple servants while their peer was treated like a princess from a fairytale. She found the clothing bulky and uncomfortable but accepted a bit of annoyance in exchange for looking regal next to her soon-to-be husband. Even as she approached the estate, she could hardly believe that what started as a single night of passion had blossomed into an unexpected love.*

*Thomas escorted Elizabeth from the carriage; she expected to find his father waiting, but the entryway was bare. She looked at Thomas with confusion but allowed him to escort her inside. Elizabeth found it strange that the house was so quiet, nary a servant to be seen. Thomas quashed her concerns, brushing it off as his father's generous nature. Thomas walked Elizabeth up the grand staircase and down a long corridor. He spoke of their love and the adventures they would have. They climbed another set of stairs at the end of a lonely hall. Thomas told her she would have grand rooms, but that she must promise one thing: to be as quiet as a mouse. He explained how his father hated noise and that he wanted her to make the best possible impression on him.*

*At the top of the stairs, he took her along a narrow hallway to a door. Scooping her up, Thomas beamed at her and pushed the door open with his booted foot. He placed Elizabeth on the soft feather bed in a room filled with all the luxuries she could ever desire—gilded furniture, silver combs, and an elaborate dressing area. Thomas explained that it would be best for her to remain there while he approached his father. When the moment was right, he would present her properly, and then they would have a grand party with all of society in attendance. Thomas kissed her, then disappeared through the door.*

*Elizabeth swirled about the room, examining every detail and amenity. When she reached the small table, she let her fingers caress each fine object. The fancy letter opener caught her eye especially; she turned it in her hand, delighted upon seeing her initials at the base of the blade. Thomas was right; the room had everything she could want.*

*In the evening, there was a knock on the door, and a male servant entered carrying a silver tray. Elizabeth's eyes roved over the sumptuous meal of meat pie, bread, and wine. "Will I not be dining with my husband?"*

*The dark-haired man said not a word as he placed the tray on the table and walked out. This time, Elizabeth heard the clicking of the lock. She ran to the door and struggled with the handle; unable to open it, she called out, "Open the door, please! Let me out!" Her pleas went unanswered, and Elizabeth's anger swelled. "I want my husband now!" Pounding on the door, she received no satisfaction. Darkness came, and with it, the door finally unlocked. Thomas stepped inside and spoke no words, only pulling her into a deep kiss. Elizabeth's anger fell away to her passion.*

*Afterward, they lay entangled with one another and through heavy breaths, Thomas promised her that it wouldn't be long before she would be presented to his father. He said that in the meantime her personal servant, William—the dark, silent man—would see to her every need. Elizabeth agreed, her worries acquiesced. Vowed days morphed into the assurance of weeks, and as time passed, her only company was William and Thomas's frequent passion. Each night he came to her, and by morning he was gone. This continued until one-night Thomas didn't come. Her heart wept. The next morning, the daily visit of food arrived. "Please, where* is Thomas? Where is my husband?" she begged the servant for answers.

The silent man placed the tray on the table and turned to leave, as he did every day. This day, he paused at the door and turned to face Elizabeth. He opened his mouth as if to speak, but no sound came.

"Can you not speak?" she asked him.

Before he could respond, the door opened, and Thomas strolled in. He motioned for the servant to leave, then slipped off his jacket, tossing it on the corner chair. Once the door closed, he pulled her into a kiss. Elizabeth pulled back this time. "Where have you been?"

Thomas smiled. "I have been tending to the future." He drew her again into his arms, his desire clear. Elizabeth took his words to mean their future and responded passionately. Morning came, and she was alone. She took her place at the dressing table and watched her reflection. She could no longer deny the soft radiance impending motherhood provided, even locked away from the sun and warm breeze. Elizabeth caught sight of Thomas's discarded coat, still lying across the chair.

She collected it, breathed in his scent, and held it to her. "I'll tell you tonight." At that moment, a letter slipped from the pocket. Elizabeth claimed the note,

*starting to replace it before curiosity got the better of her.*
*Her brow furrowed in confusion as she read the words.*
*It was an invitation to the wedding reception of Thomas*
*Chambers II and Mary Essex — that very day.*

*"He's marrying another?" Elizabeth's heart*
*burned with rage, realizing she would never have the life*
*Thomas promised, nor were there any plans for her to*
*ever leave the room she'd been imprisoned in for months.*

*Elizabeth paced, waiting for the moment she could*
*confront Thomas's lies and betrayal. It did not come.*
*Night and day came and left her bitterness to fester and*
*bloom. Her only company now was William, the mute*
*dark-haired man. He listened to all her secrets and fears*
*over the months he came to bring her food. He shook his*
*head sadly while she spoke wildly about ideas of escape,*
*none of them suitable for a common pregnant woman*
*and a penniless servant. Her fury would reach such*
*violent outbursts that oftentimes — for fear of the baby's*
*health — William would be forced to slip calming herbal*
*agents into her tea to make her drowsy.*

*The baby continued to grow, and with it, her anger*
*towards Thomas. Weeks passed, and her fire grew into*
*such a powerful need for revenge that it seemed to take*
*on a force all its own. Winter came, and with the bitter*
*cold, she cried her plea into the wind... cursing*

*Thomas's future. "You will never know the love of this child. Many little ones will come, but none will see more than your first."*

*One cold night, the door unlocked. Elizabeth was heavy with child but stood to meet Thomas. He entered, his hungry smile familiar as his eyes swept over her. A moment passed before he seemed to realize her condition. "A child?" He moved to sweep her into his arms. "That is wonderful, my darling."*

*Elizabeth pushed him away, disgusted by his touch. "You act so happy, yet would your wife be pleased to know of me or the child?"*

*Thomas' smile faltered, his eyes falling on the invitation left carelessly behind. "Well, there's no reason to pretend any longer. Careless of me. Oh well; it matters not. This is your home, and here you will stay. You and the child will be fed and cared for; what more could a whore like you expect to have in life? You're fortunate to be pampered so."*

*"I will not stay your prisoner!"*

*Thomas chuckled, the sweet smile fading from his eyes as they darkened in anger. He grabbed her cruelly by the arms and growled, "You will be a good girl and be here when I wish to see you. You see, I knew from the start my father would never approve of a common whore, no matter how beautiful her charms. It's the perfect solution. My wife has little understanding of how to please me, but you, my wild-hearted love, do." Thomas pulled her mouth to his, claiming it without love or tenderness. He arched back in pain, eyes storming with rage. "What have you done?"*

*Elizabeth stepped back, the letter opener in her hand, droplets of his blood beading along the edge. "You will never have me. To think I loved you." She watched as he collapsed back into the chair, a tempestuous smile grazing her lips as she took the letter opener and pierced her own belly. She made sure Thomas was watching as she bled out, ending her life along with the one she carried.*

*Elizabeth's body, still swollen with child, was buried in an unmarked grave on the estate. Thomas survived the injury, living on with the gruesome memories of that fatal night to haunt his dreams. His legal wife, Mary, carried many children in the years to follow, but all were lost by their seventh month, leaving the family doctors baffled as to a reason for the precisely timed complications. She grew ill from the physical and emotional tax the failed pregnancies placed on her body, and a chasm of resentment swelled in her towards her husband. Thomas's life bred only bitterness after*

*Elizabeth's passing, his days sour and empty until he was finally freed by his eventual death.*

Julia's head dropped back against the wall as she read the final sentence, unshed tears stinging at the backs of her eyes. When she was reading the words, it was as if her bedroom had disappeared and she was existing within the pages instead. Her simple bed had transformed into a four-poster antique, complete with decorative cornice and intricate enclosing tapestries. She could even smell the polished wood and see the crackling brilliance from the fireplace.

King Henry jumped on the bed to cuddle, breaking the spell. Julia reached over, absentmindedly giving his ear a scratch while she tried to make sense of it all. "What do I do? I found out who E.C. is—poor Elizabeth Chambers—but that doesn't tell me what's going on now, here in the present."

The orange tabby looked at her, pawing the pages of the book and nudging her with his large head. Then he draped his furry body over the open volume and flopped onto the surface as if he was there to stay.

Sighing in mock exasperation, Julia lifted the cat into her arms. When his soft bulk was no longer blocking her view, she cocked her head, noticing another part to the story. Unlike the original entry, this page was filled with notes, written in different inks and by different hands. Each entry described how the letter opener came to belong to different individuals, each resulting in a death. She read the entries closely; tragic tales involving death surrounded love, both new and aged. From a honeymoon ending in a bloodbath to the unconscionable murder of a spouse of 35 years, the type of victim always bore similar commonalities; they were passionate, touched by infidelity, and most times claimed they were unable to remember their crimes. Out of all of the owners of Elizabeth's letter opener, only two held the piece for many years without incident.

Julia felt dizzy and sick all at once. She'd suspected that the murder of Tom Peterson had more to do with the strange letter opener than she could account for, but never in her most outlandish dreams did she think it was connected in such an astonishing way.

She thought back to the visions she'd been having and the strange inner voice that felt foreign in her head. Aunt Sadie had said in her letter that objects could hold a piece of their owners, some sort of echo of the emotions they once felt. She had warned that some of this essence was not benign, perhaps capable of bleeding into the heart of someone new with just a simple touch.

Julia compared Tom Peterson and Thomas Chambers in her mind. Aside from their first name, the men had other qualities in common as well. Their lives may have been separated by hundreds of years, but they both shared the same wandering eye and poor impulse control. Could Elizabeth's antiquated agony have targeted Tom Peterson somehow? Could her overwhelming emotion have punished him through Julia herself?

Looking down at her hands, Julia felt almost surprised when she found they weren't stained with blood. They were trembling, however, at the thought she had been a pawn in an age-old quest for vengeance.

Julia stroked Henry, trying to still her shaking. *Does being taken over by the emotions of a scorned eighteenth-century woman absolve me of guilt?* she wondered, feeling a bit unhinged. She imagined trying to explain all of this to Sheriff Barrett, and the thought made her want to laugh out loud.

# Broken Promises

## ~ Chapter 20 ~

Julia woke, her head pounding. She sat up, rubbing her temples and trying to keep the pain from worsening. She expected to find Henry mewing for his breakfast, but glancing at the windows, she realized it was still night. The migraine wrapped itself tightly around her skull, blurring her vision slightly. She pinched the bridge of her nose, trying to clear it. That's when she noticed the pattern on the comforter—it was of roses. *This isn't right.* She ran her fingers over the smooth material. Looking around the room, everything was different. The throbbing in her head intensified. Julia's breath caught as she slid off the bed. "Where am I?"

At the window, she pulled back the heavy velvet drapes to find that it wasn't night that darkened the room, but shutters blocking out the sunlight. She backed away, ignoring the wildfire between her temples, and gasped as she fell backward. Pulling herself upright, she felt something wet and sticky on her hand. The dim lighting made it difficult to discern what it was, but the odor tinged with iron was apparent—*blood*.

As her eyes adjusted to the low lighting, she discovered that she'd fallen over a body. Blood oozed from a deep abdominal wound. Julia clambered backward, knocking into a chair. She got to her feet and ran for the door. "Help!" She grabbed at the handle, but the door refused to open. Julia pounded her fists on the door, but nobody came. "Help me! Please! Open the door!" Silence was the only response, broken by the thudding of her heart. "Please." Her voice strained as she fell back against the door. Since it seemed there was no escaping, Julia took a calming breath and stepped closer to the body.

It was a pale woman in a long, flowing dressing gown. One of her hands rested against her rounded belly, where a deep wound continued to offer blood faster than the gown could absorb it. Julia moved closer, stooping down and inspecting the woman's right hand. Her breath caught when she recognized the ornate silver letter opener. Without thinking, she reached out and pried it from the woman's death grip. "Elizabeth," Julia whispered as the blood from the blade dripped onto Julia's own nightgown.

The door to the room opened then, bathing the lifeless body in flickering candlelight. A tall man with thinning hair walked in carrying a large blanket. He didn't acknowledge Julia's presence, only stood over the woman's body. Julia watched as he rubbed tears from his eyes with the back of his hand before he spread the blanket out and gently, almost reverently, laid Elizabeth on it. He smoothed down her dressing gown before carefully wrapping her within the blanket. Before covering her face, he leaned closer and kissed her forehead. He mouthed something, and new teardrops fell, touching her cheek as he finished wrapping her up.

Finally finding her voice, Julia managed, "Please. Tell me what happened."

The man ignored the question, scooping Elizabeth's body into his arms and hefting her dead weight through the door.

"Wait!" Julia ran to follow, but when she reached the door, she was thrown back, landing on the small rug near the bed. The letter opener was knocked out of her hand, clattering to the floor and sliding across the wooden surface. Her vision blurred as the pain in her head returned, a vice squeezing her skull nearly to the point of cracking. She began to scream as she thought the pain would never end.

Julia bolted upright, and the large book tumbled to the floor in the process. She could still hear echoes of her own terrified voice as the early morning sun streamed its first light through the windows. The pounding in her head had subsided to a dull throb. She rubbed her temples, trying to ease the ache away. All of it had been a dream. *Just a dream.*

Henry bounded onto the bed. "It's good to see you, my friend." The sight of the orange tabby was like a comforting beacon of normality. Julia gave him a good rubdown, but the cat seemed oddly indifferent, nosing a small area on her nightgown instead. Julia looked down and noticed small spots of red on the cotton material. The pain in her head shrunk to an insignificant memory as she touched the fresh droplets of blood.

Julia gasped, yanking her hand back only to find the same red tinge on her hand. Her dream stormed to the forefront of her mind, causing her to remember every frightening detail. "This can't be happening. It was just a dream."

Julia crawled out of bed, her legs shaking as she stood at the bathroom sink, washing the blood off. "I feel like I'm going crazy." She didn't like the hysterical sound of her own voice. Henry came in and sat on the edge of the tub, and she looked at him in the mirror. "It was just a dream, but how did I get blood on my hand?" When the blood was cleaned away, she found a long paper cut on the pad of her index finger. The hairline wound must have been caused by one of the pages from Aunt Sadie's bound volume as it fell from her lap, unbeknownst to her. She glanced around the bathroom, feeling both silly and afraid. "Sadie, you could have shared a little more detail in your letter." After getting her hands clean, she pulled off the nightgown and soaked the stains.

An hour later, showered and sitting on the deck with her tea, Julia thought about the dream. She didn't have much choice; her mind refused to shut it off. "It must have been caused by reading about Elizabeth. My imagination is running wild," she convinced herself weakly.

She thought about the servant in the story, the one who brought Elizabeth her meals and kept her company during her pregnancy. In her dream, he had shown such care for her, and Julia couldn't help but wonder whether he'd felt that way about her in real life. Below her, people walked past towards Artists Point. She brushed it off as the music festival crowd already beginning to form, until she heard the short bursts of a police siren. "What now?" she asked aloud, a premonition of fear seizing her gut.

Julia headed inside, slipped her boots on, and made her way downstairs. Outside, she joined the flow of curious, concerned people who looked just as confused as she felt. A large crowd had gathered near the rocks before the concrete water break that created the small bay. The area could be dangerous in winter, but the locals understood Mother Nature and appreciated Lake Superior's temper. More than one visitor—from either a careless step or brazen stupidity—had slipped from the concrete catwalk and fallen several feet to the rocks below, twisting an ankle or worse, breaking a leg.

Julia snaked her way through the crowd. Seeing Jacob Prescott—from the coffee klatch at the Blue Water Cafe—standing to one side, she headed right over to him. "What's going on?" she asked, knowing that of those who could give her the scoop, he was pretty high on the list.

Jacob shook his head. "Not sure yet. My guess is someone slipped—daredevil kids or the like. Guess the festival will start with a bit of excitement."

Julia nodded, hoping all the commotion was an overreaction, but then she saw Deputy Reynolds and another officer moving the crowd back to allow an ambulance room to back in. "It must be worse than a sprained ankle. I'm going to try to get closer and check it out." She touched Jacob's shoulder as she pressed into the crowd, making her way towards Jack Barrett. He was conversing with someone down by the bay, using large hand movements and pointing directions.

"I'm sorry, ma'am, you'll need to stay back." A female officer spoke with authority. "Everyone, back it up!"

Julia looked past her. Any other moment, she would welcome the opportunity to see Sheriff Barrett, but a gnawing feeling in her stomach said something was seriously wrong. "Do you know what happened?" she asked the officer, but her voice was lost in a sea of questions and murmurs from the crowd of onlookers. She felt a bit of self-contempt, worrying that she would be lumped in with the rubberneckers. Pushing the feeling aside, she raised her voice and tried the question again.

"Well, good morning, Mrs. Crawford."

It wasn't the response Julia had been expecting, and that's when she realized she'd been so preoccupied with what was going on near the bay, she hadn't even looked the officer in the face. When she finally did, she was surprised to find it was Michelle Reynolds. Julia knew her from various bookish events around town, but the last time she'd spoken to her was during the 911 call about the break-in at Past Imperfect. "I didn't know you were a patrol officer," Julia blurted. "I didn't recognize you in uniform—it suits you."

Michelle offered a bashful smile. "I'm not normally. I work dispatch and emergency services. My husband, Sam, is the patrol officer in the family. Sheriff Barrett called everyone in to handle the crowd."

Julia gave her a puzzled look. "All this manpower for someone slipping? Doesn't that seem a bit over the top?"

Michelle lowered her voice and moved her head in close. "I shouldn't say anything, but she didn't slip. The scene is being considered a crime; it looks as if foul play was involved."

Julia's eyes widened. "What? Who?"

Michelle's eyes flickered, as if she were weighing how much she was willing to divulge. "Emily Peterson," she answered.

Julia's knees weakened. "Emily's down there?! Is she okay? Are… are you sure she didn't slip?"

Michelle shook her head. "I don't know anything about her condition. I'm sorry. All I know is I heard she got into an argument at the Gunflint last night. It seems the argument might have continued towards the lake."

"Oh my God, she's been out there all night?" Julia bit her lower lip, horrified. She imagined a bent and broken Emily suffering against the rocks in the shallow water for hours on end.

"Looks that way. Thank goodness someone spotted her when they did. Hopefully they don't have too much trouble pulling her up."

A thought crossed Julia's mind at nearly the same moment a name sprung from her lips: "Sandy."

Michelle had been momentarily distracted, ordering a couple young boys back from the restricted area. As soon as she could, she turned her attention back to the conversation, furrowing her brow and asking, "Who? What did you say?"

Julia squirmed, wishing she'd kept her thoughts to herself. "I saw Emily last night at the Gunflint. She was there with Sandy, but they weren't arguing, just talking." She intentionally left out the part where Emily seemed upset. How could the woman have been anything but with all that was going on in her life? Besides, Julia had assumed her troubled expression was mostly due to seeing her husband's so-called murderer there at the bar. Julia didn't think Emily would ever look at her the same again, even if she did turn out to be innocent and somehow manage to prove it.

Michelle shrugged. "I'm sure whatever happened will come out when the sheriff questions everyone involved. You might be called on to make a statement." She sighed and shook her head. "I sure hope things settle down, though. First Tom Peterson's murder, then someone breaks into the evidence locker, and now this. The station has never been so busy."

"Wait, someone broke into the evidence locker?" Julia didn't have to ask what was stolen, sure she already knew the answer.

Michelle nodded. "The weapon from the Peterson murder was the only thing taken. Bizarre, huh?"

Julia nodded absentmindedly. Over Michelle's shoulder, she could see that the first responders had successfully retrieved Emily and were maneuvering her onto a gurney. However, there was something odd about the gradual pace the paramedics were working at, and it took Julia a moment to notice that Emily was completely shrouded in a tarp-like material.

Emily wouldn't be transported to the hospital after all. She was heading straight for the morgue.

# ~ Chapter 21 ~

Julia floated along with the crowd, breaking off to head back to the shop. She felt numb with shock, unable to process the tragic event. "Lucy?" Julia found the young woman sitting outside Past Imperfect. She was cross-legged with her backpack in her lap, head tilted against the dark-stained door frame. "Are you all right?"

Lucy looked up, her eyes puffy from crying. Julia helped her to her feet, wondering if she could have already heard the news about Emily. "Come in and let's talk."

Once inside, Julia locked the front door, keeping the *Closed* sign up. She wasn't ready to deal with any stragglers from the stream of people outside. She led Lucy upstairs and poured them both a cup of tea. She sat down on the sofa next to her and said, "Tell me what's going on."

"I got into another fight with my mom last night," Lucy revealed. "I don't know what's going on with her. She's been acting strange for a while now. She started dating this guy named Pete. I keep asking to meet him, but she just says it's not the right time. Last night, she came home late and upset. I asked what was wrong, but she just snapped at me." Lucy's voice broke as new tears fell. "She told me that I was the reason that he left."

Julia offered her a handkerchief and gave her a moment to settle herself. "Who left? Pete?"

Lucy shook her head. "My father. My mom said she wasn't attractive to him after I was born. I guess I ruined her body and he had an affair." She dabbed her eyes again. "That's why he left. It's all my fault."

Julia frowned, pulling Lucy into a hug. "It's not your fault. People can say the worst things to each other, especially to the ones they care about most in the world. I'm sure she didn't mean it."

Lucy jerked back. "She did mean it. I know she did. She relives the whole thing every time she looks at me! She said she saw him with someone else. That he got phone calls at odd hours. I don't even think he tried to hide it."

*Another two-timing man, just like all of them.* Julia felt an angry heat rise from within her. It seemed to flare up out of nowhere, and before she knew it, she was feeling an intense fury towards Graham and every other cheating male on the planet. "Maybe he did leave her because of you," she snapped. "You can't trust a man to stay loyal."

The look of hurt and surprise on Lucy's face was like a splash of cold water. Her mouth hung open wordlessly.

Julia shook her head, horrified by what she had said. She felt a touch of vertigo as she pondered whether the words were even hers at all. "No... I didn't mean it." She knotted her fingers. "I'm sorry. It's been a bad week, and I have my own issues regarding infidelity. I think your situation just triggered some raw emotions, so please forgive me." Internally, she wasn't so sure. She had never been one to snap at someone, but her reactions were all over the place this week. Perhaps it was just the stress getting to her. It felt like the world—reality itself, even—had turned on its ear and she couldn't trust anyone. Not her friends, not the upstanding Jack Barrett, not even herself. "Lucy, marriage is hard, and your mother is obviously hurting. Things get even more complicated when you're hurt by the one person you should be able to trust. That kind of hurt takes a long time to get over, if we ever get over it at all. Sometimes, even when we think it's in the past, the littlest thing can bring it all rushing back. We end up striking out, wanting someone else to feel as bad as we do."

Lucy sniffed. "Doesn't sound very mature. It sounds very mean, actually."

Julia chuckled despite the inner battle with despair. "You're right, it's not mature. Your mother wasn't thinking when she said those things to you. Sometimes in the heat of the moment, we want things that, under normal circumstances, we'd never wish on our worst enemies. "

"What about you?" Lucy asked tentatively. "Do you wish you could take back the things that happened in your marriage?"

The question caught Julia off guard. She wasn't sure whether she was ready to open up about her personal life to this young woman, but Lucy had shared so much about herself that Julia had to at least make an attempt. She let go of a long sigh before she spoke. "In a way, I suppose. There will always be regrets no matter what choices we make. I came here because my aunt passed away, but I stayed because I needed a change. It went far beyond the state of my marriage. Sometimes you can love someone and everything seems perfect, but sometimes *because* you love someone, you don't listen to your instincts. You can be blind to reality and paint a picture of perfection with an unhappy palette. When you are away from the situation, the colors run, and you start to see what's hidden beneath the surface. That's what happened to me." Julia felt lighter. She'd never told anyone about her feelings and how it was more than Graham's betrayal. She'd betrayed herself as well. Julia shifted, pleasantly surprised to feel Lucy's hand on her shoulder.

"I'm sorry that it happened, but I'm not sorry it brought you here." Lucy's tears had dried up, a happy smile in their place.

Julia returned the expression, feeling a triumph over the internal struggle against outrage and indignation. She understood why Elizabeth had held fast to her anger. The hatred would have served as a blanket of protection. It probably felt safer than opening up her heart and putting her emotions on the line again. It would have been so easy to act the same towards Graham, hating him for eternity.

Julia pulled Lucy into a hug. "You've been one of the reasons staying was easy." She blinked vigorously before her emotions could get the best of her mascara. "Well, what do you think?" she asked after a few beats. "Are you feeling up to working in the shop today? I think we could both use the distraction and besides, with the festival starting tonight, we should be busy."

"I saw all the people." Lucy wiped her eyes again and nodded. "I'll go down and open the door."

"Thank you. I'll be down in a few minutes." Julia picked up the teacups as Lucy headed down the interior stairs. Julia left Lucy to handle the first customers while she cleaned up and fed Henry. He jumped onto the counter, mewing at her in irritation. "I know, I should have fed you earlier." She leaned over and kissed him on the head. "Well, Your Majesty, things have taken an odd turn."

Julia's conversation with Lucy had merely delayed her mind from landing in a heap of questions over Emily's death. Now that her thoughts were idle, tangled lines of inquiry rushed at her from all angles. *Did the same person who killed Tom kill Emily as well? Or are there two separate perpetrators now? Does Sandy have any clues as to what happened to Emily? They seemed inseparable the night before, and it was no secret that Sandy was incredibly protective of Emily. Did something happen between them? Why wasn't Sandy around for protection when Emily went over the guardrail?*

Julia continued to scratch Henry's head as he ate. She remembered the look Emily shot her at the tavern, a mixture of surprise, discomfort and... fear. It sickened her to think that expression marked the last interaction they would ever have. Whether Julia was innocent or guilty, the apprehension Emily felt towards her was real, and now there would be no time for apologies.

Julia's mind went to Elizabeth Chambers and her curse from long ago. These present-day murders had to be connected, as outlandish as it seemed. The emotions from that centuries-old tragedy were bleeding into the modern world in more ways than one. How would she ever stop something she didn't fully understand? Julia exhaled in frustration. "There's something else, too. I'm missing something," she said aloud to Henry.

It was then that she remembered the half coin. Heading to the bedroom, she picked it up. This piece had the stag head but was missing the doe. "Whoever was in the Peterson house must have been looking for this. And that voice didn't sound like Sandy's." She dropped onto the bed. "Besides, Sandy was outside the Gunflint when I got back into town. She couldn't have been the one I saw." She flipped the coin over in her hand. She hadn't noticed it before, but on the back was engraved TPDC4EVR. Julia smoothed her finger over the aged engraving. "TP must be Tom Peterson, but who is DC? I can't think of anyone I know with those initials."

Lucy called from the stairwell, startling Julia from her reverie.

Slipping the coin into her night table drawer, Julia headed down to help in the shop. It was quickly obvious why Lucy had called for assistance. Based on the shifty looks the customers were giving, few were interested in antiques. Julia took a breath and started greeting each customer in the friendliest manner she could muster. The morning offered a steady flow of gawkers and individuals with insatiable curiosity.

While assisting one of her regular customers, Julia overheard two women chattering about the dead body and how both murders seemed connected to Past Imperfect.

"She doesn't look like a killer," a middle-aged woman gossiped while lifting a mahogany mantle clock from its display near the window.

"What does a killer look like?" posed her female companion, who appeared somewhere near the same age. "You can't be too sure these days."

"She has a nice smile," the first woman defended. She traced her finger over the carved wood before opening the arched rear panel to examine the clockworks and chiming mechanism. "And she's got that reserved air about her." She plunked the antique back onto the shelf with a negligent force that rattled the metal hands.

Julia's internal frustration bubbled up, and she had a brief fantasy of showing the women just how dangerous she could really be.

"It's the quiet ones you have to watch out for," the second woman said with raised eyebrows.

"You're right, Lois." The veritable bull in Julia's antique shop made a *tsk-tsk* sound. "It's such a shame. I've heard she's married, but her husband isn't here."

At that, Julia slammed the drawer closed on the pine sideboard and weaved her way around to confront them. As she did, the two women were already making their way to the door and out of the shop.

As lunchtime came, tired of the revolving door of curiosity, Julia decided to close the shop for the day. "It's going to be busy everywhere in town, why don't I make us lunch here? We can turn the tables and people-watch from the porch."

Lucy grinned. "I'd like that." She bounded off to lock the front door, her blond ponytail swinging behind.

Upstairs, Julia prepared ham and cheese sandwiches, and they sat in the chairs on her deck. The late summer afternoon was sunny, but a slight chill hinted at the coming autumn. Instead of rehashing their earlier conversation, they avoided the subject and talked about Lucy's future instead. Julia was happy to listen to the young woman chat in place of being left alone with all the thoughts, fears, and unanswered questions bouncing around in her mind. Neither of them mentioned murder or the passing crowd below.

After a couple of hours, an unspoken acceptance seemed to pass between them; it was time to get back to the real world. Julia walked Lucy downstairs.

"I may be in a little early tomorrow," informed Lucy just before she left.

"That'll be great. I'm sure we'll be packed. Just use your key."

Lucy bit her lower lip. "That's just it. I can't find it," she confessed reluctantly. "The last time I saw it was a few days ago. I'm sorry, please don't be upset."

Julia was too exhausted to feel irritated. "It's all right—I'm not upset. I'll make sure to be down and have the door unlocked for you. Don't worry about it."

Lucy pulled Julia into a tight hug. "Thanks. You're the best."

Julia returned the hug, a nagging question snaking through her mind. *Was that how someone got into the shop without breaking in?* She could never be quite sure whether she had left the door unlocked on the night of the break-in. If someone had gotten hold of Lucy's key, that would explain a lot.

Julia snapped the door closed after Lucy left, running her fingers over the deadbolt while lost in thought. *Murderers and missing keys don't bode well,* she thought. *It's time I had these locks changed.*

# ~ Chapter 22 ~

Julia watched through the window as Lucy made her way down Broadway towards Wisconsin Street. Spontaneously, she decided to take a walk by the water. Her mind was a cyclone of grief and questions, none of the whirlwind helpful or productive. She was hoping that a walk might calm her nerves and give her a bit of clarity.

As soon as she made her way to the street's end, finding the oversized parking lot near the coast guard station teeming with vehicles, the day's tragedy rushed back to her in full force. The chaos-filled morning left her mind in such a spin that she'd almost forgotten about Emily. Now, as she neared the point where the woman's life had met a dreadful end, Emily was all she could think about. First her husband was murdered, and now she was dead. An entire household wiped away. Even though Julia had only known Emily a few months, she had considered her a friend and would miss her.

Julia paused near the coast guard warning sign. Farther beyond, she noticed the yellow police tape around the fatal area, and it took her some time before she managed to slip past unseen and towards the wooded area of Artists' Point. Visitors usually used the stairs up to the break before heading right to the lighthouse or left to the large, flat rocks that made up a well-known part of Artists' Point. She stepped along the faint trail, careful not to misstep in the vining roots, before coming out on the edge of the rocks.

All summer, the area was filled with vacationers wanting to explore the rocks or take in the view of the lake. Today, though, it was quiet, the blue-green water lapping foamy waves against the base of the rocky land.

*A dead body will do that.*

Julia welcomed the solitude but couldn't feel any enjoyment from the eerie calm. Lake Superior was subdued, much like her bottled-up emotions. Julia would eventually grieve with the incoming tide, but for now, she would be satisfied with the gentle rhythm that helped settle her thoughts. She climbed onward, towards the farthest point, only to discover that someone already occupied the outcropping—a lone woman sitting cross-legged facing the lake, her shoulder-length black hair moving in the breeze.

Julia started to turn back when she heard, "It's all right," and the woman gestured for her to join her.

Julia was surprised to find that the woman was Sandy. She hadn't recognized her from behind. "I hope I'm not intruding," Julia said apologetically. "We seem to have had the same idea."

"I'd like the company," Sandy said wistfully. She shifted over and offered the space next to her.

Julia wrestled with the offer, out here all alone not far from the place Emily met her demise. Sandy might have been the last one to see her alive. Would she be safe up here next to this woman? Her arms prickled with goose bumps as she weighed the danger in her mind.

*Is she safe next to **you**?*

Julia pushed her fears aside, crouching down and taking the spot next to Sandy. It wasn't until that moment that she could see how red and puffy the woman's eyes were. Julia pulled a linen handkerchief from her skirt pocket and offered it to Sandy. "I'm sorry about Emily. I know you two were close."

Sandy took the cloth, an ironic smile forming as she wiped her eyes. "Thanks. I can't believe she's gone." Her voice broke on the words, and she stared down at her feet while her shoulders shook.

"Neither can I." Julia looked away politely while the other woman sobbed. "It's been a strange week. Like something out of a bad mystery novel."

Sandy looked at Julia, the corners of her mouth pushing up a bit. "You can say that again. I wish I'd followed her when she left the tavern."

Julia tentatively squeezed her shoulder, her curiosity piqued. "It isn't your fault."

"Isn't it? We got into a stupid argument and she stormed off. She always liked the beach. I never thought she'd go out on the break at night. If I had been with her, she wouldn't have slipped."

"You can't know what happened." Julia gave her most comforting expression. "Is that what the police think? That it was just some horrible accident?"

Sandy squinted, looking insulted. "I don't know what they think. What else could it have been? You sound just like the sheriff. I spent most of the morning answering questions for him."

"You spoke with Sheriff Barrett?" Julia asked. "What sort of questions did he ask you?"

Sandy gave a ragged sigh in time with a wave as it lapped against the edge of the large slab. "I don't know… different stuff. He wanted to know how Emily seemed last night and who she was with. She wasn't well—I told him that much." Sandy pulled her knees up, wrapping her arms around them, chin resting on her forearm.

Julia knew she was treading on thin ice, but she couldn't stop herself from saying, "During all the commotion, one of the officers told me there was reason to suspect Emily was pushed. Do you have any idea why that would be? Was there a witness who heard a scream or an altercation? Something like that?"

Sandy glared at Julia. "How should I know?"

"I'm sorry, I just…"

"No," Sandy straightened up and waved a hand in the air as if she could sweep the words away. "*I'm* sorry. I'm not myself right now. I haven't wanted to think about it, I guess. There was something about a wound on… her body."

Julia raised her eyebrows.

"I overheard the sheriff and deputy talking about it," Sandy explained. "I don't really know any more than that. When they noticed I could hear them, they clammed up."

Julia was quiet as she let the information settle in.

"She was such an amazing person," Sandy said, filling the silence. "Even when we were in school. Damn, I just wish the last things we said weren't in anger." She sniffed back tears.

Julia nodded, unsure of how to comfort her. "I can understand that. No one wants to end things on a bad note." She wanted to keep her talking. "What was Emily like in school? That's where you met, right?"

Sandy nodded. "I knew Tom since we were kids. Our fathers worked for the lumber company on the Gunflint. He was always one to get into trouble—not that I was much different then. But then I met Emily. Her family moved here when she was in the ninth grade. She was so shy, but smart. I just wanted to protect her from the world."

Julia smiled at the shift in tone when she changed from speaking of Tom to Emily.

Sandy chuckled. "I convinced her to try out for a bit part in the spring play. I told her it would be a great way to make friends. She would only do it if I tried out too. She ended up with the lead, and I built sets." She sighed. "I didn't care. I loved to hear her sing. She had a beautiful voice."

"I didn't know she sang. I love music, though my singing voice isn't ready for any stage."

Sandy snapped her head towards Julia. "Don't say that. I've heard you. You have a wonderful voice." A blush colored her cheeks as she looked away.

"You've heard me?" Julia didn't know whether to be flattered or nervous.

"I like to walk along the lake early in the morning—you know, before the city folk wake up. I've walked by the shop and heard you."

"Oh." It was Julia's turn to blush. She was in the habit of singing while completing mundane chores. She hadn't considered how well her voice might carry through open windows in the stillness of dawn. "I like the quiet of the mornings, too. You should stop by and have a cup of tea sometime." Julia knew she was getting off track. She wanted to gather all the clues she could, and instead she was playing at making new friends.

Sandy nodded, distracted. "I should have tried harder to stop their relationship before things got serious with Tom. He was never good enough for Emily."

"You mentioned he was unfaithful, even then," Julia gently prodded.

"Yeah. He didn't give Emily two glances when she first came to school, but the summer before our junior year, she blossomed. He was already going steady with Dorothy Cooper, but suddenly he couldn't keep his eyes off Emily." Sandy tossed a small rock into the water. "She wasn't pretty enough for him before, but things changed that summer. He kept visiting her father's shop; they used to own the store where the mercantile is now."

"He had a girlfriend but pursued Emily?"

Sandy gave Julia a weird look—an odd mix of bemusement and disbelief that somehow expressed, *Are you kidding me?*

Julia felt a rush of heat spread into her cheeks, realizing how naïve she sounded. "I just meant about his pursuing her openly, even though he wasn't available." She cleared her throat. "He must have been pretty bold."

Sandy snorted. "That's because Dorothy wasn't around by then. Her family spent that summer travelling around the States. The only way she would've found out was if someone had told her later." Sandy stared out over the lake, her mind taking a trip back in time. "You know, I'm not even sure she knew that Emily was the reason he finally broke up with her. Anyway, when school started, they were a couple and Dorothy was old news."

"It had to be hard for her to see them together." Julia sighed, watching the water.

"It wasn't easy for anyone involved—then or later. I guess poor Dorothy got over it when she married Mike Wells. They seemed happy for a while, but even that ended. Maybe we aren't meant to be happy." Sandy wiped her eyes with the embroidered cloth again.

Without thinking, Julia squeezed Sandy's shoulder once more, moving her hand over her back. "I don't believe that."

Sandy shifted as if the touch burned her.

Julia pulled her hand back. "I'm sorry." Her fingers knotted together in her lap. "I should go."

Sandy's silence confirmed her suggestion. Julia stood and started her trek back across the rocks. She stopped after only a couple of steps, a thought occurring to her. Turning back, she called, "Sandy, were you talking about Dottie Cooper, Lucy's mother?"

Sandy didn't look back, only nodded.

Julia couldn't believe it had taken her that long to put together that Dottie was a common nickname for Dorothy. Her mind turned with this new information as she continued across the rocks, music from the festival dancing on the air. She climbed back along the gravel path and headed into town towards the sheriff's office.

# Chapter 23

"How can I help you?" The older woman at the front desk was a bit frazzled, the small-town precinct probably busier than it ever had been.

"I'd like to see Sheriff Barrett, if I may?" Julia wondered if she should have called ahead of time and made an appointment.

"You and the rest of the town," the woman said with a chuckle. "He's with his deputies at the festival. I'm afraid he won't be back here until morning."

"Of course." Julia mentally kicked herself. Jack Barrett had a murderer on the loose and a large crowd to control on top of it. "I'm sorry you're stuck inside. Will you get to enjoy any of the festival?"

The woman laughed. "I attended the festival years ago, when I had less silver in my hair. You should be out there enjoying it yourself."

"You're right, I need to get out there. You don't know, by chance, where Sheriff Barrett might be at the festival?" Julia gave a shy smile, hoping the woman would be more forthcoming.

"He said he was going to cover the area near the bay where the main stage is." She shrugged. "That's about all I can tell you."

"Thank you—that helps." Julia turned to leave.

Before Julia reached the door, the woman called out to her, "If I were twenty years younger, I'd be out looking for him, too."

Julia smiled back over her shoulder as she left the station and made her way back into town. The quarter mile stretch of Highway 61 was alive with other pedestrians. She passed the restaurant, My Sister's Place, before taking the opportunity to cross the two-lane highway. Turning left, toward the lake and Wisconsin Avenue, she smiled whistfully at the lights and many festivalgoers. Music and happy chatter filled the air. The shops, normally closed by now, were awake with their doors propped open. Any other moment, Julia would have been excited to enjoy an evening during the special event, walking among the artisans' pavilions and tables, making sure to stop by and get a bit of Beth's fudge. She glanced down Broadway, spotting her darkened shop. It was supposed to be open. She'd planned to dress in a beautiful antique dress and serve passersby tea and scones. *Next year.* Entering the merchant area that lined Broadway, Julia watched for the sheriff while greeting friends she'd made over few months she'd been there.

"Now why don't you have a table out here?" Simon, the owner of a small shop on Wisconsin Avenue, chided Julia playfully.

Stopping, Julia replied, "I didn't have a chance to get things ready, but I'll be more prepared next year. Save a spot next to your table."

Simon not only owned a shop, he headed up the merchants' association. He had a brilliant mind for organization and planning. "I'll hold you to it."

"I promise." Julia flashed a warm smile. "Hey, have you seen the sheriff?"

A teasing smile played on Simon's lips. "Looking for someone to watch the fireworks with?"

Julia blushed a deep crimson. *Was everyone a matchmaker in this town?* "Not exactly. We haven't even had so much as a cup of tea."

He laughed. "More than one relationship has started under those colorful lights. Besides, he's been alone too long."

Julia just smiled. "Have you seen him? I really need to speak with him."

"Last time I saw him, he was headed towards the bay."

"Thanks. I'll catch you later." Julia slipped into the crowd before Simon could offer any more relationship advice. She walked past her sleeping shop and turned towards the bay. The boats, usually anchored during the summer, were lit with lanterns, offering a colorful display.

"Julia!" a voice called from somewhere in the crowd.

Julia saw Lucy running over to her, and for a moment, she thought something might be wrong. "Is everything okay?"

"Yeah. I came with some friends." Lucy jerked her thumb over her shoulder in the direction of a group of young adults. "I just wanted to say hi and… well, I wanted to thank you for being there for me… you know, earlier today. I was kind of a mess."

"Sweetie," Julia exclaimed, her heart touched, "I'll always be there for you." *If I'm right, you're going to need the support.*

Lucy pulled her into a tight hug. "Thank you," she said, her voice muffled against the fabric of Julia's blouse.

Over Lucy's shoulder, Julia caught sight of Jack Barrett. He wore a serious expression along with his full uniform, and he was chattering into his shoulder walkie-talkie. Julia asked Lucy, "How about we talk tomorrow? There's someone I need to speak with."

"Sure. I'll be there. Enjoy the festival." Lucy ran off, joining a mixed group of what looked like young college kids.

"I hope I'm wrong." Taking a deep breath, she headed off to where she'd spotted Jack. The bandstand was in the open area in front of the bay, and a large crowd had gathered. Julia worked her way through it, but a strong hand on her right arm halted her progress. She tried to pull her arm back, but the clamp held fast. "Excuse me." She looked to her right. Dottie Cooper glared at her. "Mrs. Cooper. Are you all right?"

The smudged mascara said she wasn't. "I won't let you do it."

A flash from one of the stage lights glinted off something Dottie was holding. Julia's eyes widened, seeing the missing letter opener in her hand. "Mrs. Cooper, I think we should sit down and talk."

"We're going to. Now, go on." Dottie shoved Julia towards the lake, away from the crowd.

"We can go to my shop. It's close by." Julia's voice broke against her attempt to stay calm.

"Shut up and keep walking." Dottie pressed the tip of the blade against Julia's side for emphasis.

Julia winced at the brief pain in her ribs. She quickly nodded her compliance and walked in the direction her captor indicated. As they moved forward, every possible escape idea flashed through her mind, each more ludicrous than the one before. The sharp pressure against her side, however, reminded her that escape without injury was unlikely.

Passages from Aunt Sadie's books came to mind, swirling bits of information that suddenly formed into one cohesive revelation. Dorothy Cooper wasn't acting on her own emotions; she was acting on those left over from Elizabeth Chambers. She was a victim of the curse, stripped of rational thought and therefore dangerous and completely out of her mind.

Julia was feeling a bit giddy as they left the grassy area and crossed the parking lot near the boat launch. The fact that she was being threatened by Dottie with the letter opener allowed her to let go of her own guilt, the fear that she herself had committed those terrible wrongs. Relief was a strange emotion to feel over learning a dear friend's mother was a deranged killer, but Julia couldn't help but find comfort in the proof of her own innocence.

The parking lot was packed with cars, but there were no people to be seen. The point had been closed earlier in the day, so no one was there to take advantage of the privacy Artists' Point offered at night. Julia's hopes trickled away the farther they got from the festival crowd.

"We're heading to Artists' Point. The woods," Dottie informed her in a hollow tone of voice.

"Mrs. Cooper… Dorothy, you don't have to do this. I can help you." Julia's words sounded small and infantile, even to her own ears.

"You've helped enough," Dottie snapped, pushing Julia towards the steps that led up to the water break. "Go left." She pushed again, and Julia stumbled forward, scraping her leg on the concrete wall.

Julia pulled herself up and made her way back towards the woods. She'd been there only a few hours before, deep in discussion with Sandy. She'd give almost anything to rewind the clock now.

"That's far enough," Dottie said gruffly when they had nearly reached the same outcrop of rock where Julia sat earlier.

Julia stopped and turned to face Dottie. The evening had darkened, but there was still enough fiery light left along the lake's horizon to see that Dottie's expression was full of rage and pain. This was the same mix of feelings Julia had felt when reading the story of Elizabeth Chambers. It may as well have been the woman herself instead of Dottie standing before her now.

"Please." Julia spread her hands out wide, an idea occurring to her. "Elizabeth," she addressed her. "You don't have to hurt anyone anymore."

Dottie didn't miss a beat. She brandished the letter opener close to Julia's face. "What do you know of hurt?"

"I know you've been hurt." Julia kept her voice soft. "You loved someone who betrayed you. Someone who forced you to betray yourself. That is the worst betrayal of all."

Dottie shook her head madly. "This is all your fault. You came here and tried to steal everything from me!"

Julia mentally tripped on the bump Dottie just threw at her. "I don't know what you're talking about. I would never steal from you."

"So, you're going to deny it?" Dottie flaunted the blade again. "All I ever hear is Julia this and Julia that. When she was little, she wanted to be just like me, and now, it's only you."

Julia was flabbergasted. "You mean Lucy? Dottie, she's just a friend. You're her mother. I couldn't and wouldn't want to take your place. I promise."

"You're lying! It wasn't enough for you to take my little girl, you had to take him, too?" The blade glinted in the final ribbon of light piercing through the trees.

"Wait. Who are you talking about?" Julia thought quickly, "You mean Tom Peterson?" Julia's head spun as she navigated the curvy road of Dottie's rage. "I didn't take him."

"What would you call murder?" shouted Dottie.

"What?!" Julia grasped the sides of her head, unable to keep up with the twists in conversation.

"Don't deny it. You stole my Lucy and then you killed Tom."

Julia took a breath, trying to bring Dottie back to herself. "I didn't kill Tom Peterson. You did."

Dottie sounded surprised, speaking through a grimace of pain, "I... I would never hurt him. I loved him."

"But he didn't love you back, right? He betrayed you." Julia took a chance, uncertain of how Dottie would respond.

"He did." She glanced down for a moment, then leaned forward, pushing Julia back a step. "Yes, I gave him my heart, my everything, but then he threw it away and wanted HER!" She moved the blade closer to Julia's heart. "You've been hurt as well; you hide away from it here. Lucy told me all about it." She pressed the tip of the blade against the skin above Julia's heart. "I'll take away your pain." Dottie's scattered anger focused to a razor's edge.

Tears burned trails down Julia's cheeks. She wanted to help Dottie and in turn, the essence of Elizabeth, but she couldn't deny that the truth of those words stung. She *had* been hurt and she'd been hiding it away for years. The relief this woman promised her was enticing—sparkling like a lure amidst a sea of despair. She could feel her muscles relaxing, giving in to her fate.

"It'll be over quickly," Dottie soothed.

The words jolted Julia from Elizabeth's archaic grasp. "Is that what you said to Tom before you killed him? Did you pretend you were doing him a favor before you carved into him?"

Dottie's brow knitted tightly. "What?" She seemed to be fighting a dense fog, probably the same one Julia was struggling against.

"The morning Tom Peterson died. You were there, weren't you? You killed him."

Dottie shook her head, clearly rattled by the accusation. "No. It wasn't me. I was there the night before. We had a fight in the basement. I left before Emily got home."

Julia couldn't believe what she was hearing. She didn't trust it was the truth, and the blade against her chest did nothing to improve that feeling. "You're saying you didn't break into my shop and steal the letter opener, then use it to kill Tom—the man who betrayed you?"

Dottie's eyes narrowed. "So I'm an intruder *and* a murderer according to you? You're a piece of work. Especially since you're the one who must have killed him."

"I didn't kill him. Why would I?"

"I told you," Dottie shouted, "to hurt me!"

"Why would I want to hurt you? I don't even know you." Julia again tried to reason with her. "Look, why don't we go back to the shop and talk? We can work this out."

"No!" She positioned her arm to strike Julia with the blade.

"Dottie, no!" From behind a nearby tree, Sandy rushed towards them. She grabbed for Dottie's arm, toppling both Dottie and Julia to the ground. The impact knocked the letter opener from Dottie's grasp, causing it to land on the ground near Julia.

Dottie sat up, holding her head and moaning as if she were waking from a dream.

Julia scrambled to her knees and crawled to Sandy. The woman wasn't moving, lying in a lifeless heap on the ground. "Sandy?" Julia cradled Sandy's head in her lap. Blood oozed from a gash on her forehead. Julia searched her pockets, then remembered she'd given Sandy her linen handkerchief. She spotted the corner of it peeking out of Sandy's pocket. Julia pulled it out and gently pressed it against the gash.

"How'd we get out here?" Dottie asked, horrified.

"I'll tell you, if you tell me what happened the morning Tom Peterson died," Julia bargained.

Dottie's brow furrowed. "I'm not sure."

"You went to his house, didn't you? You dropped this." Julia pulled the cut coin from her pocket and showed it to Dottie.

In the low light, Dottie had to come near to examine the pendant. "He gave that to me before my family went away the summer before our senior year. He swore to never take his half off, but he wasn't wearing it as soon as we came back, and he was already chasing Emily."

Bitterness fell with each word. "I threw mine at him when we argued the other night."

Julia continued to put pressure on Sandy's gash, her palm feeling warm and sticky. "Is that when you decided to break into my shop and steal the letter opener to kill him?"

A twig snapped. "She didn't kill anyone." Lucy stepped into the clearing, leaning down to claim the letter opener from the brush it had fallen into.

"Lucy?" Julia felt a rush of relief. "Sandy needs an ambulance—do you have your phone on you? Call nine-one-one and then go get Sheriff Barrett, he's by the main stage. We can talk through everything later."

Lucy didn't jump to action the way Julia had expected. Instead, her neutral expression hardened into something fierce. "No. You'll send my mom to jail," she said. "She doesn't deserve it; she didn't do anything wrong."

"It's okay," Julia assured her in a trembling voice. "We'll work it all out, but right now you need to get help. Sandy needs help."

"I'll get the sheriff when I'm done," Lucy said coldly.

"Done? What are you talking about?" Realization was dawning in Julia's mind, but she didn't want to believe it.

"Lucy, honey, what's going on?" Dottie stared horrified at her daughter, who was now holding the letter opener in a death grip.

"It's okay, Mom. I won't let anything happen to you."

"Lucy, what did you do?" Julia asked calmly.

Lucy turned her angry stare back to Julia. "I did what I had to do. Tom Peterson was a liar and a cheat. I found out what he did to my mom and why my dad left."

"Honey, no..." Dottie started to cry. "It was my fault. I was so twisted up about him. I've wasted so much time and energy on that man, but at least something beautiful came from it. You."

"He deserved it. He betrayed you with her! He should have married you and made it right!" Lucy cried, her grip tightening on the handle.

"Honey, please." Dottie buried her face in her hands.

Lucy shifted her foot, advancing towards Julia and Sandy.

Julia was trapped, unable to leave Sandy in order to escape. She could only watch the young woman approach helplessly. "Lucy, I'm your friend. Please, it's all right. We can work it out and get you help."

Lucy's free hand went to the side of her face. "I… I don't want to hurt you. You're my friend." Her voice sounded strange and hollow, and her grip faltered just enough for the blade to slip from her hand.

"Freeze!" Jack Barrett's deep, commanding voice cut through the air. He stood, gun drawn, just inside the small clearing. "Are you all right, Mrs. Crawford?" He didn't move his eyes away from Lucy as he spoke, keeping his gun level with her chest.

"Yes, but Sandy is hurt," Julia called.

The sheriff ordered Lucy to the ground before he pulled his phone from his hip, pressed a single button, and started barking orders. The evening was tipping into the darkness of night as he cuffed the young woman. "Lucy Wells, you're under arrest."

## ~ Chapter 24 ~

Julia sat at the desk staring at the picture of her Aunt Sadie. The chaotic events of the last week played out in her mind. After everything that had transpired, she wrestled with the idea of closing the shop and going back to the Cities. After thinking on it all night, the apricot sunrise over the lake begged her to stay. "I'm not like you," she whispered to the picture. "You had a fire I just don't have."

The ringing of the brass bell over the front door ended her one-sided conversation. Julia was pleasantly surprised to see the broad-shouldered, uniformed man on her doorstep. "Sheriff Barrett," she greeted him.

"I wanted to stop by and see how you were doing this morning." His polite tone wove easily around her ears.

She smiled at his kind gesture and motioned for him to come inside. "I'll be all right. It'll just take a little time to sort through everything. Can I get you a cup of tea or coffee?"

Jack shook his head. "No. Thank you, though. I checked with the hospital, Ms. Edwards should be released in a day or two. They kept her for observation. She took a nasty blow to the head."

"I'm glad Sandy will be all right." Julia dropped her gaze to the floor sadly as she added, "I just hope Lucy will be."

"It will be up to the DA as to what happens criminally speaking. She confessed to stealing the letter opener but couldn't explain why. Her memory is fuzzy... doesn't remember being in the Peterson house, but her fingerprints were found in the living room." Jack took in a deep breath, moving his head slowly from side to side. "The whole thing is baffling, to say the least. What she does claim to remember is strange. She had some crazy story about being held prisoner by a man and carrying his child. I think it boils down to some severe mental issues coming to light."

Julia nodded, trying to keep her expression in check. "She needs help. I just wish she wasn't alone in dealing with everything. I'm not sure her mother is in any state to be strong for her."

"She'll get the help she needs and don't worry, she won't be alone. Her father, Mike, is on his way now."

Julia's brow knitted. "Are you sure that's a good idea?"

The sheriff smiled. "Why wouldn't it be? He's her father and Lucy and Dottie will need him now."

Julia snapped, "But he abandoned them…"

Jack's relaxed posture stiffened. "You don't know what you're talking about. Mike is a good man. I've known him both professionally and personally for years."

Julia snorted. "Good men don't leave their family and have affairs."

The sheriff bit back, "And women shouldn't jump to conclusions without having all the facts. You don't even know half the story." He blew out a frustrated breath and changed the subject. "Either way, Lucy admitted to stealing the opener from the evidence locker, and we know she was there when Emily died. She remembers following Emily out to the Point soon after she saw her talking to Sandy at the Gunflint. Memory or not, it isn't hard to piece together what happened after that. The puncture wound in Emily's back tells how it ended. It seems there has been bad blood between her mother and Emily since high school."

"Some betrayals aren't so easily forgotten."

The sheriff didn't respond, only stared at Julia. He started to speak but seemed to think better of it.

Julia felt heat flush through her cheeks under his unwavering observation. "Um… what about Dottie?"

The comment broke through the momentary tension, and he softened his gaze. "That's up to you."

"Me?"

"Sandy said Dottie threatened you with some sort of weapon, like a knife—"

"She's mistaken," Julia interrupted. "It was dark." She knew Dottie hadn't been herself, but how could she possibly explain to the sheriff that she was under the influence of an otherworldly force?

The sheriff studied her face as he considered her words. "Then why were you at the Point?"

"She needed to talk," Julia lied, thinking fast. "She was afraid something was wrong with Lucy and wanted my help in figuring it out." *Enough people have been hurt in this.*

Jack Barrett held his belt buckle, a dubious expression playing over his face as he shifted his hips to redistribute the weight of his duty holster. "Then you won't press charges?"

"No." Julia shook her head firmly. "There's nothing to charge her with."

The sheriff shrugged with a look of surrender. "We were unable to find any weapon at the scene, so I'll have that file closed."

Julia tried not to let the relief show through in her smile. "Thank you."

"We also haven't been able to find the missing weapon: the letter opener of yours that was stolen from the station and also matches the wound on Emily Peterson. It wasn't found in the Cooper residence. I've got men searching the area just in case. It's possible she dropped it in the lake so that we'd never find it."

Julia met his eyes and nodded, trying to appear convincingly disappointed. "I hope they find it. It's a priceless antique."

Silence fell between them, and just as Julia was beginning to fear the sheriff's suspicion, his phone rang, piercing the quiet. Jack grabbed it and said, all businesslike, "Barrett. Yeah, be right there." He disconnected and clipped it back on his hip. "I need to get back." The tension faded in his tone as he reclaimed the gentle command Julia found attractive.

Julia followed Jack to the door, watching from the display window as he drove away. She sighed as she engaged the deadbolt and switched the painted sign to *Closed*. Turning, she scooped up Henry and cuddled him a bit as she strolled to the back of the shop. She deposited Henry on the desk, saying, "Well, Your Majesty, everything seems to be settling down. Just one more problem to take care of." Julia opened the desk drawer. She pulled back the corner of her linen handkerchief, still spotted with Sandy's blood, to reveal the now dulled and dirty letter opener.

Henry mewed almost accusingly, narrowing his large oval eyes.

# Chapter 25

Music filled the air, the atmosphere upbeat and celebratory. Few attendees knew of the events of the previous night, but the announcement that the killer had been apprehended added to the enjoyment of the residents.

Julia sat on the floor of her flat. A fire crackled in the fireplace, and Henry curled up beside her as she meticulously cleaned the letter opener. She wore her white curator gloves as she ran the polishing cloth over the sharp edge. Once done, she placed it on the floor in front of her. "Well, Henry, I'm not sure if this will work, but it's all I know to do."

The large orange tabby bumped his head against her leg and purred.

Julia peeled the gloves off and discarded them. Slowly she stretched out her fingertips to touch the letter opener. Instantly she felt a pull from it, a desire that wrapped around her as her fingers twisted around the cool metal. Julia slowed her breathing, trying to keep her mind clear and allow whatever she felt to move through her. The energy was unmistakable and strong, but it only flowed through her like a fleeting current. "How did touching this send Lucy to kill Tom Peterson?"

Julia turned the blade in her hand, her eyes falling on the insistent indention left by her wedding band. Her brow furrowed as images of Graham flashed like an old slide projector in her mind. Each image excavated long-buried feelings of hurt and anger. The energy wrapped around her, feeding off her anger at his betrayal.

*"He hurt you, Julia. You deserved better than that."* There it was now, the voice. For so long she had feared the words had come from somewhere within, but now she recognized it for what it was: the remnants of Elizabeth Chambers and her fury.

An image of Graham laughing while talking to someone on the phone played out as she stared at the flat surface of the blade. She could hear him so clearly; it was the same laugh she used to love when they first started dating, an attentive, melodic sound. She never heard him laugh like that with anyone else, always saving that special sound for her alone... until that dreadful phone call.

*"He lied to you. You knew what was happening—what's still happening."*

"No." Julia tried to force her thoughts away from Graham.

*"He betrayed you. He told you he loved you."*

"I know, but..." The anger surged, images shifting from true memories of things Graham had said and done to those she'd only imagined—*an unfamiliar blonde rolling to face him in bed, kissing his bare chest as he laughed delightedly.*

Julia remembered arguing with Graham, and suddenly she could see herself pushing him away when he tried to apologize. "You lied to me! Don't deny it." She viewed herself as if she were watching a movie, pulling her arm back, the letter opener tightly in hand as she brought it down to stab Graham in the chest.

Julia gasped, dropping the blade, her breath short, heart pounding. Looking at her hands, she saw they were covered in blood. "No. It's just an illusion. Not real."

"You can make it real. Make him pay for what he did to you."

Julia whipped her head around as she looked for the voice. "Elizabeth?"

The room was silent, cut only by sharp, shallow panting from Julia. Henry was still next to her; he bumped his head against her leg again, purring. She knew they weren't alone.

"Elizabeth, please. I know he convinced you to give up the life you had, promised you everything, and then took it from you. He was wrong. You hated him for it."

"Yes." Elizabeth appeared, eerily pale, with blood on her gown and her hand resting on the baby bump beneath.

"You hated yourself more. Hated yourself for not seeing who he really was." Julia didn't have to puzzle out Elizabeth's feelings; she knew them all too well.

Elizabeth only stared at her, pain and anger haunting her eyes. Slowly, she began to speak. "He did more than lie to me. Men always lied, made promises never to be kept."

Pain spread like fire; Julia held her head and squeezed her eyes shut, willing the agony away. Slowly it faded, and when she opened her eyes, she stood in the room where Elizabeth died.

"He was different. The devil himself."

"He got you to betray yourself... to ignore all the warnings you felt and give yourself to him anyway. He convinced you that your own feelings couldn't be trusted. He got you to doubt yourself."

"He was like all the others, but worse."

"Not all men are like that."

Elizabeth snorted. "After all that was done to you, you still believe in them. You have been hurt once but are willing to risk yourself again. You are a fool."

"You are blinded by your own hatred. You've forgotten someone."

At that moment, the door opened. A lean man stepped into the room, a tray in hand. On the tray sat a silver dome, a pitcher, flatware, a rose, and a book. He set the tray on a small table and prepared it as if he stood in a dining hall.

"William," Elizabeth whispered. It was the first time any emotion other than loathing had graced her ghostly face.

"He meant something to you," Julia ventured.

She nodded. "He was my jailer... my confidant... and my friend. When Thomas first locked me in this room, before I realized it was my prison, William would tell me about the manor house and when Thomas was a child. It made the times Thomas was gone easier to bear, for I truly loved Thomas and wanted us to be happy."

Julia watched as Elizabeth moved closed to William. "The day I discovered Thomas's betrayal was also the day I discovered how cruel he could be. To ensure William's silence, he had his tongue removed." Elizabeth's eyes closed, an expression of pain coloring her features.

Julia's eyes widened.

"I knew there was no hope for any of us."

"Did you know William loved you?"

Elizabeth turned, uncertainty in her eyes. "What do you mean?"

"William may have lost his ability to speak, but he still told *your* story. He came in and tended to your body and tried to give you the dignity in death that Thomas took from you in life."

Elizabeth turned to face the fire. After several moments, she said, "He wept."

"Yes, I saw him wrap your body with great care. It was obvious that he loved you."

"He should have helped me escape." Bitterness crept back into her tone.

"How? Do you think you would have been able to get far? Even with help, what means did he have? You knew a secret... you *were* a secret. One Thomas couldn't risk anyone knowing about. Imagine what he threatened to keep his sins quiet. William had already suffered at his hands, so he must have been terrified for your safety. Perhaps he would have figured it out eventually, but you gave up on him too soon. Even so, you weren't lost to it all. Not to him." Julia glanced down; the letter opener was no longer on the floor.

Elizabeth turned, holding it as she had centuries before. "The path is burned into being. I cursed it and sealed it in blood."

The tears that burned Julia's eyes fell. "It doesn't have to be. He told your story. Yes, Thomas lied and betrayed you, but William refused to allow you to just be discarded. He wept for you and your baby. Your curse worked; Thomas was the last of his line. His life was full of sadness and loss. But it didn't stop there, and your anger has destroyed many other lives, too. Please stop this before it goes any further. Let go of the hate and anger now before it consumes anyone else."

Julia thought of Graham, his image rushing to the forefront of her mind. She hadn't heard from him since his surprise visit. Sadly, she wasn't upset by it. Before all the events of the last week had happened, a part of her hoped he would just appear one night, a changed man, and whisk her back to the Cities. She wanted him to promise her everything and for things to be like they were before, but better. But now, Julia realized she didn't want to live that fantasy. She wasn't even the same person, and the way their relationship was before wasn't what Julia wanted.

Julia thought about Jack Barrett. Was he her white knight? Did such a thing even exist? She didn't want to be like Elizabeth and give up on a happily-ever-after.

"Mistress Elizabeth."

Both Elizabeth and Julia turned to see William watching them from the table—not simply the shadow of a memory. "He can't hurt you anymore. I've been waiting for you to return and be free of it all."

"William, you can speak again. How is this possible?"

"All he took in life can be returned to you in death. Release the anger binding you to your hate."

"I… I cannot forgive."

"Thomas or yourself?" Julia interjected.

Elizabeth gripped the ornate handle tightly, railing against Julia. "Do you forgive your own betrayal?"

Julia furrowed her brow, staring at the fireplace. Turning back, she replied, "I have to. I don't want to lose my life to hate and anger, and it isn't too late for you, either."

"Please, Elizabeth. I've waited so long to see your beautiful smile again. Leave this place with me." William extended his hand.

Elizabeth's hand dropped to her side, releasing the letter opener. It clanged against the stone tile that made up the hearth area. Her skin no longer held the unhealthy gray hue, and the crimson bloodstain on her gown faded until the material gleamed a pure white.

Julia felt a strong rush of wind and dropped to the floor, buckling against the blast. Once the gust passed, the anger was gone. Catching her breath, she looked to where Elizabeth and William had been standing, but they were gone. She found herself looking at her own living room. The letter opener still lay on the ceramic tiles.

Henry crawled onto Julia's lap and snuggled against her, purring.

She started to pet him but pulled her hand back, remembering the blood. It was gone. She cuddled Henry close to her chest, allowing her tears to fall. Henry kissed over Julia's face with his rough tongue. She laughed, feeling him parent her.

After Julia's face was cleaned to his satisfaction, he mewed and sauntered to the deck.

Julia sat, staring at the letter opener. "I can't just leave it there." She reached out, touching it tentatively. She felt only the smooth surface. Taking a deep breath, Julia closed her fingers around the handle. She no longer felt the energy or the rage. "It worked." Relieved laughter spilled out. "I don't believe it, Aunt Sadie. I did it." Julia grabbed the cleaning cloth and carefully cleared away her fingerprints, but the blood she saw earlier was no longer there.

She smiled, hearing the music on the main stage change to jazz. She nestled the letter opener back in its original box. The velvet cover was still missing. She padded across the living room to the bedroom and placed the box at the bottom of the wooden chest at the foot of the bed. Julia put everything else back in place and secured the latch.

She shawled her favorite afghan around her shoulders, poured a glass of wine, and walked out to find Henry curled up on one of the Adirondack chairs, enjoying the cool breeze and good music. Julia sat in the other chair, looking out over the water, allowing the music to fill her. She knew the sun would come up the next day and she would still have to deal with Graham.

It was time to stop running from the past and embrace it and herself. Julia sipped her wine and smiled, hearing the crowd applaud the band.

She was home.

## Author Bio

Anne has always loved the North Shore, especially Lake Superior near Grand Marais. When bringing the Past Imperfect series together, Anne couldn't think of a better place to have Julia's shop. If you find yourself traveling through, stop by Artists' Point, you may just find her sitting on the rocks.

Anne loves to meet and chat with her readers. You can connect with her through the links below.

Subscribe for exclusive details and free books:
https://www.annewillowauthor.wordpress.com

Stop by and chat:
https://www.facebook.com/annewillowauthor

Follow on Twitter:
https://www.twitter.com/cozymysteryanne

Thank you, for sharing your time with me. I hope you enjoyed Julia's first adventure.

Anne

# Broken Promises

Anne Willow

Made in the USA
Monee, IL
06 December 2020

51204665R00152